I0720779

SUBSTITUTE BRIDE

MARGERY SCOTT

Copyright © 2016 by Margery Scott

All rights reserved

ISBN: 978-1-988191-03-4

This is a work of fiction. Names, characters, places and incidents are the product of the author's imagination or are used fictitiously. Any resemblance to actual persons, living or dead, events or locales is entirely coincidental. Any trademarks, service marks, product names, or named features are assumed to be the property of their respective owners, and are used only for reference. There is no implied endorsement if any of these terms are used.

No part of this book may be used or reproduced in any manner whatsoever without written permission of the author except in the case of brief quotations embodied in critical articles and reviews.

MARGERY SCOTT'S BOOKS

HISTORICAL ROMANCES

MORGANS OF ROCKY RIDGE
Travel to Rocky Ridge, Colorado and meet the
Morgan men
and the women who love them.

Cade

Trey

Zane

Will

Jesse

Brett

Heath

ROCKY RIDGE ROMANCE
It isn't only the Morgan men who fall in love in Rocky
Ridge.

Landry's Back in Town
Substitute Bride
Wanted: The Perfect Husband
Hannah's Hero

High Stakes Bride
Jasper's Runaway Bride
Mail-Order Melanie

MAIL-ORDER BRIDES OF SAPPHIRE SPRINGS

Miranda

Audra

Kathryn

Elise

Laura

Cassie

OTHER HISTORICAL ROMANCES

Emma's Wish
Wild Wyoming Wind
Rose: Bride of Colorado
Mail-Order Melanie

ROMANTIC SUSPENSE

A Time for Secrets
No One to Tell
The Stranger She Knows
A Question of Guilt
A Stranger in Paradise

MEDICAL ROMANCE

The Surgeon's Homecoming
Stranded with the Surgeon
The Firefighter and the Lady Doc

CONTEMPORARY ROMANCE

Winterlude

CHAPTER 1

*E*lizabeth Main's heartbeat stuttered as the postmaster handed the battered envelope to her twin sister, Sarah. It had been six long years, but Elizabeth recognized the barely legible handwriting immediately.

Cole. Cole Berringer's scrawl.

"It's from Cole," she exclaimed, her insides abuzz with excitement. "Who is it addressed to?"

"Me, of course," Sarah replied. "Although why he'd write to me now after all these years, I have no idea."

Elizabeth closed the door against the perfumed breeze from the honeysuckle arbor in the yard and the rattle of carriages passing on the cobblestone street outside. Her skirts swished on the polished wood floor as she followed on Sarah's heels through the foyer.

Sarah crossed to her father's study and retrieved an engraved silver letter opener from his desk, then strolled into the drawing room and sat daintily on a brocade chair beside the fireplace.

Elizabeth followed close behind, barely able to contain herself. She'd waited for this letter since the day he'd ridden away to fight in the war so long ago.

"Open it, Sarah," Elizabeth urged, and a moment later, added, "What does it say?"

"Patience, Bee." The reprimand was softened by the smile on Sarah's face. "I haven't read it myself yet."

Elizabeth bristled. She remembered the day Cole and Quinn had given her the nickname, and it had stuck until Cole left for the war and his brother had followed shortly after.

"I really wish you'd stop calling me Bee," Elizabeth said. "We're exactly the same age, and nicknames are for children. We're grown now."

Sarah chuckled, the soft musical tone so unlike Elizabeth's own hearty laugh. "I'm sorry, sweet. I forget how much it bothers you that I'm four minutes older than you are. Will you forgive me?"

Elizabeth met Sarah's blue-eyed gaze and smiled. She'd never been able to stay angry with her twin for more than a minute or two. And she was much more interested in what Cole had written than she was in continuing her pique.

While Elizabeth paced the room, Sarah opened the envelope, then withdrew three pieces of paper and began to read.

Elizabeth watched the play of emotions on her sister's face as her eyes scanned the paper—a tiny frown, a faint smile, her teeth worrying her bottom lip. She couldn't stand it a second longer. "Well? What does he say?"

Sarah looked up, her eyes wide. "He writes of all that's happened to him since the war, of his success as a rancher."

"A rancher?"

Elizabeth had been heartbroken when Cole hadn't come home after the war. A neighbor who'd returned a few months after the war ended had told her he'd gone to Colorado, but no one had heard anything about him since.

Sarah nodded. "Yes. He and Quinn own a cattle ranch, over ten thousand acres."

Elizabeth couldn't even imagine so much space. Why, the ranch was likely larger than Summerton, the small town outside Philadelphia where she and Sarah had grown up.

"What else?" Elizabeth prodded.

"He wants me to come to Colorado. He wants me to marry him. Look." She held up a fistful of ten-dollar bills.

Elizabeth couldn't prevent the gasp that escaped her lips. Cole and Sarah? Married? If someone stabbed a dagger into her heart, it couldn't cause such pain, she was sure. In fact, she suspected her heart had stopped beating altogether. She could hardly bear to ask the question, but she heard herself voice the words. "Will you?"

The silence in the room was punctuated by the hourly chime of the grandfather clock in the corner. Elizabeth's throat grew so tight she feared she'd soon be unable to breathe.

Sarah smoothed the crumpled pages and folded them neatly, then slipped them back into the envelope. Before she had a chance to respond, the door burst open and an elderly woman rushed in. "Who was at the door?" she asked, fanning herself furiously against the July heat.

"The postman brought a letter from Cole, Aunt Meg," Elizabeth told her.

"Cole Berringer?"

The disdain in her aunt's voice surprised Elizabeth. What did she have against Cole?

Elizabeth nodded. "He wants Sarah to go to Colorado and marry him. He even sent money for her travel expenses."

"Good heavens." Aunt Meg's fan quivered like a hummingbird's wings. "That's…that's preposterous…"

"He's doing very well financially," Sarah put in.

"He's no better than that drunken father of his." Aunt Meg practically spit the words out. "I'm astounded at the nerve…writing after all this time…as if people had forgotten what happened and why he went off to war in the first place."

"I'm sure he's grown up by now," Elizabeth interrupted. "It was a long time ago." And not entirely his fault, she could have added, but decided sometimes silence really was golden.

"Hmmph. Nevertheless, you can't make a silk purse from a sow's ear." Her aunt had a proverb for every situation, and Elizabeth couldn't remember ever getting through a conversation without hearing at least one. "Has anyone ever tried?" Elizabeth asked innocently.

Her aunt's face reddened. "What...?"

"Maybe Sarah could turn Cole into a silk purse." Elizabeth couldn't imagine Cole being any different from how she remembered him—tall, strong, with eyes the color of slate and a tiny dimple in his chin that she'd teased him about for years. No, she couldn't picture him as a refined town gentleman, sipping tea with the ladies or dressed in a frock coat and derby.

Aunt Meg let out a bitter laugh. "The wilds of Colorado are the perfect place for the likes of him. He'd fit right in with the rest of the ruffians who headed west after the war."

Elizabeth was tempted to point out to her aunt that it was 'ruffians' like Cole, men who craved adventure and who were willing to risk their lives to explore new frontiers, who had discovered America in the first place. "I think he was very brave—" she began.

Aunt Meg scowled at Elizabeth. "Of course you do."

Elizabeth suspected this was part of the reason she'd fallen in love with Cole so long ago. She'd known it the first time she'd seen him that he was the only man she'd ever love. Of course, he'd been little more than a boy then, poised beside the Ring-the-Bell, his shirt sleeves rolled up, his sinewy forearms gripping the mallet, and a cocky grin on his face. In one smooth effortless arc, he'd swung the mallet. She'd watched as it had hammered the board at the bottom, sending a piece of metal flying up a tower. A moment later, the bell had rung. Right then, she'd fallen in love, and even though her heart had been shattered when he'd begun courting Sarah, her love for him had grown stronger with every passing day.

And then he'd left Summerton. Gone to fight for the Union Army. She'd prayed every night for his safe return, and even though he hadn't come home when the fighting was over, at least he'd been alive.

Sarah's voice interrupted her reverie. "I wonder if there are shops in Colorado."

Elizabeth could have given a two-hour lecture on Colorado. She'd read everything available on western travel and settlement, as well as the tales in the dime novels she hid beneath her mattress.

Aunt Meg harrumphed. "The whole idea is ridiculous. Why, I've heard about the west—outlaws, Indians who capture women and…well, never mind…"

Sarah smiled up at her aunt and tucked the letter into the pocket of her skirt. "Don't worry, Aunt Meg. I have no intention of going off to Colorado."

Elizabeth heard the sigh of relief escaping from her lips and guiltily slid a glance to her sister and aunt. Had they heard her?

"Good. At least you have the good sense to stay where people are civilized and you'll be able to marry a man who'll be able to look after you properly and treat you like the lady you are." Aunt Meg closed her fan and turned away. "Now, let's forget all about this Colorado nonsense. Tea is ready, and we still have many plans to make for the ball next month."

"Eighty-seven, eighty-eight…" Elizabeth stifled a yawn as she sat at her dressing table later that night and ran the mother-of-pearl hairbrush through her long blonde hair.

Suddenly, the door burst open. Sarah hurried in and let out a distressed sigh as she flopped down on the bed, her frilly chemise and pantaloons flapping.

Elizabeth turned from the mirror to face her sister. "What's wrong? Is Aunt Meg trying to marry you off to old Lucius Grant again?"

Sarah grimaced and gave an exaggerated shudder. "I don't understand why Aunt Meg is so insistent I marry him. Why not you? It's not as if he'd even know the difference."

"I don't understand it either, but I admit I'm glad I'm not the target of her matchmaking at the moment. After her attempts to marry me off to Edgar Whitting-ton, only to discover he has a wife and children tucked away in the country…"

"That was unfortunate for him, but providential for you," Sara put in.

"It was, and since then, Aunt Meg has allowed me time to recover from my broken heart." Elizabeth began to laugh, and within seconds, she and Sarah were lost in a fit of giggles.

When they finally composed themselves, Sarah gave Elizabeth a stern look. "The problem is that since you've escaped her clutches for now, she's turned her attention to marrying me off. I'm almost tempted to marry Cole just to avoid Aunt Meg's matchmaking."

Elizabeth's throat tightened. Surely Sarah wasn't serious. She'd made it very clear earlier that she'd rather wither away as a spinster than live in the Colorado wilderness.

"But even marriage to that fuddy-duddy couldn't convince me to go to Colorado. Cole has been out in the sun too long if he thinks I'd ever consider his proposal," Sarah said, running her braid through her fingers.

"But you were sweethearts," Elizabeth said, as if she needed to remind Sarah of her relationship with Cole. "You must have loved him."

Sarah waved away Elizabeth's comment. "He loved me, and I must admit I was flattered by his attention. He was very handsome, after all. But love? Heavens, no. Can you imagine being married to a man like Cole? And worse, living on a ranch in the middle of nowhere?"

Yes, Elizabeth thought, her mind wandering. She'd imagined just that for years. Well, not the ranch part, but she had fantasized about being married to Cole and living with him in Colorado every night after she said her prayers.

Now, she could add a ranch into her imaginings along with space, fresh air, land. Working beside him on his ranch, raising his children, building a life together. Her heartbeat quickened at the thought. If only Cole had loved her instead of Sarah. If only the letter had been addressed to her…

"I'm going to bed," she announced, slamming the brush on the silver tray on the dressing table.

Bounding up, she crossed the room, slipped out of her silk wrapper and draped it across the foot of the bed. Sliding under the sheets, she turned her back on her sister lest she see in her eyes the longing for something she'd never have. "Please turn down the lamp before you leave," she muttered as she pulled the blanket over her shoulders and closed her eyes.

Hours later, Elizabeth's eyes sprang open. The house was silent, the fire had died, and faint moonlight filtered through the curtains at the window.

An idea had germinated somewhere in her subconscious as she slept. She and Sarah were twins. They'd spent many hours giggling about how they'd fooled not only their parents, but the servants, their tutors, their friends.

Why not Cole? Could she fool him, too? Her heart skittered inside her chest. It was a dangerous plan, one that could ruin her reputation and leave her homeless.

Yet, excitement gnawed at her at the thought of becoming Cole's wife.

Sarah didn't love Cole, so Elizabeth's actions wouldn't hurt her. Sarah would never leave Summerton. So why couldn't she take Sarah's place and make her own dreams come true?

There was no doubt in her mind that what she was considering was wrong. Yet if it made Cole happy to think she was the woman he loved, and she was married to the man she'd dreamed of for years, how could it really hurt anyone?

She'd loved Cole since the day she'd discovered the difference between boys and girls, and her prayers that he'd somehow discover he loved her, too, had gone unanswered. Now, this opportunity had presented itself, an opportunity to make her dreams come true.

Yes, it was deceitful, and she was sure her plan was a sin, but the temptation was too strong to resist.

She would go to Colorado. She would become Sarah. And she would marry the man she'd always loved.

"What in blazes are you doing?"

Cole Berringer looked up from where he was squatting beside the trail leading into Rocky Ridge. The noonday sun silhouetted his brother, Quinn, still astride his cocoa brown gelding.

"What does it look like I'm doing? I'm picking flowers."

"That's what it looked like, but I thought I was having hallucinations." He dismounted and wandered over to stand beside Cole. "Any particular reason, or you just have a sudden yen for posies?"

"They're for Sarah," Cole said, his insides heating with anticipation of her arrival. "According to Cammie Todd at the mercantile, a woman should have flowers at her wedding. I want everything to be perfect for Sarah since she agreed to travel all this way to marry me."

"Always knew the woman didn't have a lick of sense," Quinn teased.

Cole gave his brother a withering glance. "I've waited for six years to marry Sarah, and in a few hours, she'll be my wife. I must admit I was a bit surprised when I got her letter and she said she'd be arriving so soon. From what I remember about her, I expected she'd want to spend a few weeks shopping first."

"It's possible Bee made her see the light about spending her days in the shops," Quinn commented with a grin.

Cole laughed. "Bee should have been born a boy, I think. She had no interest in clothes or doing her hair, and I remember her cringing at the thought of spending the afternoon with her aunt doing embroidery. She was always much happier climbing trees and burying her head in those dime novels she used to read instead of learning to sew and play the pianoforte and…I hate to say it, becoming a lady like Sarah."

"Do you remember the day her uncle caught her playing mumblety-peg with you behind the farrier's house?" Quinn asked. "I think he was more furious that she was playing a boy's game than the fact she could have seriously injured herself with that knife."

The memory of Bee's face—her eyes brightening and her cheeks flushing when she threw the knife and it stuck into the ground only a fraction of an inch from her shoe—filled Cole's mind. "She beat me, too."

"Her uncle was so angry I thought his head was going to explode," Quinn added.

"It didn't stop her, though. She was never one to let society dictate to her," Cole mused. "I wonder if she ever grew up."

"Likely not. And honestly, it was kind of refreshing to come across a female who wasn't obsessed with frippery, don't you think?"

Cole had to admit he'd always enjoyed hearing about Elizabeth's antics, and even though it would have been inappropriate at the time to tell her so, he admired her spunk. Still, unless she'd changed dramatically, she'd keep any man who married her on his toes. He'd be in for an interesting—but definitely not peaceful —life.

"It's strange, really," Quinn put in. "For two people to look so much alike, Bee and Sarah were complete opposites in nature."

Cole grinned at the memory of Elizabeth and Sarah each doing their best to change the other, and both failing miserably. Dragging his thoughts back to the present, he got up, his hands filled with wildflowers. "Whatever the reason Sarah was in such a hurry to get here, I'm happy about it," he said. "She's obviously just as anxious as I am to start our life together."

Now that Sarah had consented to be his wife and share his life in Colorado, all the back-breaking labor, sweat—and even blood—he'd shed over the past six years to build the Berringer Ranch had been worth it.

Elizabeth stepped out of the stagecoach in front of the Wells Fargo office and joined the four other passengers who had traveled from Denver with her—an elderly married couple visiting their son and his family, and a mother and daughter who planned to also settle in Rocky Ridge.

She squinted into the sun baking the parched earth under her feet. All around her, people scurried about, horses and wagons rolling by without a glance at the coach.

The journey had been such an adventure, and even though the accommodations had been less than desirable, the food had been barely edible, and every muscle in her body ached. And she'd enjoyed every moment of it.

The spectacular scenery and the new friends she'd made along the way had made the trip something she'd remember for the rest of her days.

The only dark cloud in the bright future she was looking forward to was the sadness and concern her family must be feeling at the way she left—at night, with little more than a valise and a small trunk holding her most precious possessions. She'd left a note explaining what she was doing and why, and she'd stolen Cole's letter from Sarah's dressing table so they couldn't write to him and tell him the truth. She only hoped they would understand and one day perhaps forgive her.

Her wayward thoughts, and the guilt she couldn't seem to shake, filled her mind as she gazed around her new home.

One main street ran the length of the town, with false-front buildings lining both sides and boardwalks in front of each, raised a step or two from the dirt. She was eager to explore the town, but right now, her stomach was aflutter at the thought she'd be seeing Cole again after so many years.

Then she saw him, standing with his brother only a few yards away. A tiny gasp escaped her lips. He was even more handsome than she remembered. His dark chestnut hair was longer now, brushing the collar of the blue chambray shirt he was wearing. His skin had bronzed, and his strong, square jaw had filled out, the cleft in his chin a little more pronounced.

And he was larger now, both in height and breadth. He was no longer a boy, but a man! A man who made her heart trip inside her chest.

Her gaze slipped to the broad shoulders beneath his shirt and lower, to the gun belt resting on his black trousers. A gun!

Of course, she'd heard about violence in the west, but somehow she'd never imagined Cole carrying a weapon.

Before she had time to muse on the other ways he might have changed since she'd seen him last, he met her gaze. His dark brown eyes widened and his lips spread in a smile as he nudged Quinn, said something to him and hurried forward to meet her.

Without a word, he pulled her into his arms and held her tightly, her body molding against his hard length. He lowered his head toward hers.

What was he doing? Was he really going to kiss her, right here on the street, in public?

And then…all thought disappeared like a wisp of smoke in a strong breeze.

Heavens! He was kissing her. He was really kissing her. And it was everything she'd ever wanted. Everything she'd ever dreamed of. And more. So much more.

She clung to him as he drew her even closer, her arms circling his waist, her hands clutching at his shirt.

And still, the kiss went on until, finally, he tore his mouth away from hers.

His breathing was ragged, matching her own. She gazed up at him, his dark brown eyes ablaze. He appeared dazed, stunned, as if he'd suffered a life-altering shock. She suspected he'd find the same expression in her eyes.

"It seems absence really does make the heart grow fonder," he murmured into her ear.

Elizabeth gazed up at him, her brain barely able to form a coherent thought. "Why do you say that?"

"You've never kissed me quite like that before. You were so much more reserved before."

She'd have to be more careful to hide her feelings

for him. She was Sarah now, and she had to remember that. "I…"

"But I like it," he added, his lips quirking in a smile. "A lot."

"Oh…" Her brain refused to function, and further speech escaped her.

"How was the journey?" he asked.

"Long, but so exciting." She turned to her new friends, surprised to find that the elderly couple had already disappeared. "Don't you agree?"

The younger woman nodded, and Elizabeth took her hand, pulling her forward.

"Cole Berringer, I'd like to introduce Delia Moore and her mother, Cornelia. They're going to be settling here, too."

Cole nodded a greeting, taking note that neither of the two women had offered their hand. "I'm happy to meet you both."

"I'm sure we'll see you again," Delia said. "Sarah and I have become friends, and I'm looking forward to spending more time with her."

Cornelia hooked her arm around Delia's. "We must be going, Delia," she said, her expression stern. "Goodbye."

Cole's brows lifted once the two women had walked off. "They're your new friends?"

Elizabeth sighed. "Delia would be, if her mother would let her, but I have a feeling she's firmly under her mother's thumb and she isn't allowed much freedom.

She reminds me of…" She paused, tightening her lips to stop herself from saying Sarah's name instead of her own. "Elizabeth and I with Aunt Meg."

Suddenly, a deep male voice interrupted. "You two going to stand there all day putting on a show or are you ready to go get hitched?"

Elizabeth's cheeks burned with embarrassment. She spun around to see Quinn approaching. He was a shorter and leaner version of Cole, and almost as handsome. She gave him a broad smile. "Quinn! It's so nice to see you again."

His gaze slid from the top of the forest green hat perched on her head to the tips of her shoes. "Good you see you, too, Sarah."

A twinge of guilt shot through Elizabeth. She'd have to get used to being called Sarah, at least until Cole fell in love with her and she could tell him the truth. But even if he never loved her the way he loved Sarah, she could live with that. Couldn't she?

For the first time, doubts began to creep into her mind. Would her love for him be enough? Could she spend the rest of her life married to Cole, bearing his children, growing old with him, knowing she wasn't the woman he wanted?

Harboring her secret until the day she died?

"Are you ready to go get married?" Cole asked Elizabeth. "The preacher's waiting at the church whenever we're ready."

"Now?" He expected her to get married without

even a few minutes to compose herself? "You mean I won't even have time to change, or brush my hair, or—"

He gave her an apologetic glance. "Sorry, but the stage was late getting in and everybody's waiting."

Everybody? "What do you mean, everybody?"

He grinned. "Folks out here don't get much time to enjoy themselves, so a wedding is a chance for them to get together and celebrate. I'd bet most of the town is already at the church. And those that aren't will be waiting for us back at the hotel."

"Oh…my…" She felt the blood drain from her face, and her heartbeat fluttered in her chest. Her vision clouded, and for a few terrifying moments, she thought she might swoon at his feet.

"What's wrong?" he asked, wrapping an arm around her shoulder as she sagged against him.

"So many people…"

"You never used to worry about being looked at. Has that changed, too?"

Elizabeth had forgotten about Sarah's ability to make herself the center of attention and how much she reveled in it. Elizabeth, on the other hand, was quite content to blend into the background and stay out of the limelight. "Perhaps it has. I've grown up over the past six years. I'm sure we've both changed."

"You're right. We've both changed." He sent her a dazzling smile. "And I'm looking forward to getting to know you all over again. Getting to know *all* of you."

Elizabeth's face heated. She knew exactly what he

was referring to. Heat swirled through her veins, settling low in her core. The tingling sensation was unfamiliar, yet most pleasant. And even though the thoughts that ran through her mind were highly improper, she admitted to herself she couldn't wait to get to know all of him, too.

"I reserved a room at the hotel for tonight, but I'm sure Mr. Avery won't mind if you use it now."

"Mr. Avery?" Elizabeth asked.

"The owner of the hotel."

"Oh."

"And nobody will mind if you take a few minutes to get ready," he added. "Most folks have chores to get back to, though, so you can't dally too long."

Elizabeth nodded. "That's fine."

Cole cupped her elbow and began to lead her down the boardwalk toward the hotel.

Once he had her settled in a room, he kissed her again and grinned. "I'll go over to the church and let everybody know you're here so they don't get too restless. I'll be back to get you in fifteen minutes. I can't wait any longer than that to make you my wife."

CHAPTER 3

True to his word, Cole knocked at the hotel room door exactly fifteen minutes later.

"Are you ready?" he asked when she opened the door to admit him.

Elizabeth looked up at him, at the anticipation, the desire and…the love in those dark depths. Love for Sarah, not her.

She'd known he loved Sarah, but now, seeing that love and hope and the promise of a bright future with her shining in his eyes, Elizabeth realized she'd made a terrible mistake. Her impulsiveness had brought her more than a thousand miles to marry him, and her love for him had convinced her that he would love her back, eventually.

But the truth was, he didn't love her. Never had, and likely never would.

As the reality of it all sank in, her heart felt as if it was falling into her stomach, and her body chilled.

"No." The word came out as little more than a breath. "I can't…marry you."

Cole's face paled. A muscle in his jaw pulsed and a furrow appeared between his eyes. "What?"

"I want to…so badly…"

He moved a few steps closer to her, his eyes boring into hers. "I know this is a rush, and you're nervous about it, but—"

"No. It's not that. It's—"

His voice grew low, sharp. "It's what, Sarah?"

Tears of sorrow for a dream that had died stung her eyes. "It's…" she choked out.

Cole gripped her shoulders, his gaze dark and intense. "Say it, Sarah. Why can't you marry me?"

Misery covered Elizabeth like a shroud. The next words she uttered would destroy the life she'd dreamed of for so many years. "Because I'm not Sarah," she murmured. "I'm Elizabeth."

His hands dropped to his sides and he stared at her for what seemed an eternity, stunned. "What?" he asked. "You're Bee?"

"I'm so sorry." She reached out to rest her hand on his forearm, noticing how pale her fingers were against his sun-bronzed skin.

He jerked his arm out of her reach and turned away from her as he raked his fingers through his hair. Then he crossed the room and paused, his hand on the door knob.

Elizabeth didn't speak. What was left to say? She'd deceived him, and she'd ruined any chance that one day, he'd see her as something other than his true love's sister.

Finally, he turned to face her. His hardened gaze swept over her as if he was seeing her for the first time. "I don't understand," he said, his voice laced with disbelief. "Why would you do this? Why didn't Sarah come?"

How could she tell him how Sarah felt about him?

Even though he had no feelings for her, Elizabeth couldn't bring herself to cause him more pain if she could avoid it. She suspected the agony in his expression was a mere hint of what he was suffering inside. She understood exactly how he felt.

"She didn't want to leave Summerton." That much was true, and she could see no reason to rub salt into his wound by telling him how Sarah had ridiculed his proposal.

"I see." Cole crossed the room and gazed out to the street below. Sounds of activity filtered through the window into the silence inside.

Elizabeth had no way of knowing what thoughts were running through his mind. He was angry. That much was evident by the way he was standing at the window, his back ramrod-straight and his hands clenched at his sides.

She resisted the urge to go to him, to apologize once more for her deception and the pain he must be dealing with. Instead, she stood quietly, her hands clasped together.

After what seemed like an interminable amount of time, he turned to look at her. His face appeared to be set in stone, his dark eyes glittering. "Why didn't Sarah write to me and turn down my proposal?"

Elizabeth was taken aback by the question, although it was a reasonable one. She just wasn't quite sure how to answer it. But she'd told enough lies, and she would not add to them. She'd tell him what he wanted to know, as kindly but as honestly as she could. "I'm sure she planned to. She just…" Sarah had tucked the letter into the drawer in her dressing table and had never looked at it again. She'd never known that Elizabeth had responded in her place. "I took the letter."

He nodded in understanding. "I only have one more question," he said. "Why did you come instead?"

Elizabeth almost reconsidered her promise to herself to be honest, but he deserved a truthful answer. "I came because…"

He gazed at her expectantly, a frown creasing his brow. "Because what?"

Oh, how she wanted to tell him her deepest feelings —that she'd fallen in love with him the first time she'd seen him at the fair. That he'd filled her thoughts and dreams since that day. That she'd lived in fear when he'd marched off to war, and that she'd been devastated when he hadn't returned.

But even though she'd always been blunt and not at all diplomatic, the words stuck in her throat. Instead, she forced a lightness into her voice she didn't feel and let out a short laugh that sounded brittle to her ears. "Because I wanted to escape Aunt Meg's matchmaking, and I decided that if I was going to be forced to marry, I might as well marry someone I know and have an adventure at the same time."

That was the truth. Sort of. She'd wanted to avoid her aunt's attempts to marry her off, and she'd always craved adventure. And yes, she could even justify her comments about marrying someone she knew. She had wanted that. She'd just avoided telling him the *whole* truth.

Her face burned at the half-lies slipping from her lips, but whether or not he noticed, she couldn't tell. His expression didn't change, and again, silence descended upon the room.

Why didn't he say something? What was he thinking?

Cole turned away from Elizabeth, emotions surging through him. Anger, bitterness, and hurt. Pain unlike any he'd ever known tore at his insides as if they were being ripped apart.

Sarah hadn't come. She didn't love him. Everything he'd done since the war to build a home for her had been for nothing.

He'd had so many plans, had dreamed about their life together, the ranch that would grow and become a legacy for the children they'd have, growing old with her by his side.

She'd told him she would wait for him. He'd written, but she'd never replied to his letters. "That's why she didn't respond to my letters."

"She didn't get any letters from you. Not until the last one, that is," Elizabeth said.

The postal service between the Colorado Territory and Pennsylvania was unreliable. "I assumed that was why she never responded. It didn't occur to me that she'd stopped loving me." He'd been so blindly in love that he hadn't given that possibility any thought at all.

And now, when everything he wanted should be within his grasp, he had nothing.

He ran his hand through his hair as he turned back to the window and looked out to the street below.

Life was going on as usual, he thought absently, as if all his plans and dreams hadn't just been smashed to smithereens.

He glanced toward the edge of town where a field dotted with wagons and horses stood outside the church, waiting for him and Sarah to arrive.

What was he supposed to do now? Dammit, he

wanted a wife. He wanted children. Wanted someone to share his life with.

Suddenly, Quinn's voice bellowed through the closed door. "Are you two going to be much longer? The preacher wants to get home in time for supper."

Cole turned and gazed at Elizabeth, sympathy and regret shining in her blue eyes. Was she sorry she'd come? Sorry she hadn't married him before she admitted her deceit?

"We're coming," Cole called out.

Elizabeth moved to stand directly in front of him. A frown creased her delicate brow. "What are you doing? Now that you know the truth, there's no reason—"

"There is," he insisted, his voice suddenly cracking. The pain of loss settled in his chest, stronger than the urge to rant at Elizabeth about her deceit. "There is."

"What? You intend to humiliate me in front of the entire town?"

"I could do that," he pointed out, "but do you think I'm that cruel?"

She stared deep into his eyes. "No, you were never cruel, and I can't imagine that changing. But then why—?"

A plan floated around in his brain and before he had time to reconsider, he said the words that would change his life forever. "Didn't you say you wanted an adventure? That you planned to pretend to be Sarah for the rest of your life?"

"Well, not forever," she admitted. "That is…" Her face colored and she nibbled on her bottom lip.

Strange, he thought. Sarah had often worried her lip that way whenever she was unsure of herself. He'd never noticed Elizabeth doing the same thing until now, but it wasn't surprising they might have the same habits.

Elizabeth's voice was barely a whisper when she spoke. "I didn't think—"

He let out a bitter laugh. "Have you ever thought anything through before you jumped right in?"

"Why…of course…"

His brows arched. "Really?" he asked. "I can think of at least a dozen times off the top of my head that you did something and regretted it because you hadn't stopped to consider the consequences. How many times did I hear the words 'I didn't think' come out of your mouth? Are you telling me you took the time to really think about what you were doing? We both know you couldn't have because if you had, you would have realized what a terrible idea it was."

But wasn't he about to do the same thing? He wasn't giving the idea bouncing around in his brain time to settle so that he could calmly and reasonably make a decision.

"As you said, you wanted an adventure and to escape your aunt's matchmaking," he went on. "I want a wife and I want children, eventually. Since I can't have the woman I love, it makes no difference to me who I marry. So, since you came here to marry me, we're going to the church and we're going to get married."

When Cole helped Elizabeth out of the wagon in front of the church at the edge of town a few minutes later, she was trembling so badly she was sure she'd crumple to the ground at any moment. "Please say something," she pleaded. "You don't have to do this. I'll go back to Summerton…"

"We're getting married. It's what you wanted, isn't it?"

"Well…yes…but—"

"Then let's go," he said, gripping her elbow and urging her forward.

The small church sat on a patch of dirt surrounded by blue spruce trees that seemed to reach straight to heaven. Three stairs led to the arched door, open and waiting for them to arrive.

A young woman holding a bunch of purple, white and yellow wildflowers waited at the bottom of the stairs. She smiled as Cole and Elizabeth approached.

"Thanks, Cammie." Cole took the flowers from her and offered them to Elizabeth. "These are for you," he said. "I wouldn't have thought of it myself, but Cammie told me women should have flowers so I picked these on the trail between the ranch and town."

"They're beautiful," she said, her voice cracking with emotion. He'd picked the flowers for Sarah, not her. Tears threatened, and she had to blink several times to keep them in check.

Cammie introduced herself to Elizabeth. "We'll talk later," Cammie said with a grin. "I have so many stories I could tell you about him…" She let her voice trail off, then turned and hurried inside.

On wobbly legs, Elizabeth let Cole escort her into the church. He'd forewarned her, but even so, she couldn't prevent herself from sucking in a shuddery breath when she saw that every pew was full.

Hushed voices followed her to the front, where the preacher waited. "Welcome to Rocky Ridge," he said, his smile soft.

Elizabeth remembered little else throughout the ceremony. At the preacher's prompts, she repeated her vows, and even though she heard the deep timbre of Cole's voice, his words didn't register in her brain.

Then it was over, and the preacher was telling Cole he could kiss his bride.

He cradled her face in his large work-roughened hands and brought his mouth to hers. This time, his kiss was a mere brushing of his lips against hers. Yet the sensation was as if her lips had been seared.

He drew away and gazed down at her, sorrow and resignation in his eyes.

But even through the guilt crushing Elizabeth, her

heart sang. She was married! She was Mrs. Cole Berringer!

Everything would be fine. She'd be the best wife he could ever ask for, and soon, he'd love her as much as she loved him.

He just had to!

Cole drained the glass he held in his hand, then put it down on the gleaming wood bar in the hotel ballroom. He gestured to the bartender for a refill as his eyes focused on a bubble in the bottom of the glass, watching it burst and disappear as if it had never existed.

His dream of a life with Sarah was like that bubble. Gone. And now, he was a married man, but married to the wrong sister.

What the hell had he been thinking? What kind of madness had taken over his brain when he'd found out the truth? He never made decisions without considering every angle, every possible consequence. Until now. And today, he'd made the biggest decision of his life without thinking about it for more than a few minutes.

He shouldn't have been surprised at Elizabeth's actions. She'd always gone ahead and done whatever she felt like doing, regardless of the consequences. Her impulsive nature had gotten her in trouble time and again when they were growing up, but it had never quelled her spirit.

A part of him—a very small part of him—had to admit he liked that about her. She'd always been eager to take part in any scheme he or Quinn had come up with, whether or not it was acceptable to society.

They'd had fun when they were young, and if he was being completely honest with himself, he'd enjoyed spending time with her as much as he had with Sarah.

But Elizabeth wasn't the type of woman a man married. She was irreverent, impulsive, and when she was angry, the object of that anger was never left in doubt about how she felt.

Whereas Sarah was a lady who knew her place, who would be the perfect hostess for a successful business-man, and who would never speak or act out of turn, Elizabeth would lead a man a merry dance. Any husband of hers would never know what she had in store for him next.

And now, in one of the very few times in his life he'd been impulsive himself, he'd gone ahead and married her.

He slid a glance at the makeshift dance floor where Elizabeth was twirling in the arms of Elias Todd, the owner of the mercantile. Even from the other side of the ballroom, Cole could see her porcelain skin was flushed with exertion and her bright blue eyes were sparkling in the light from the crystal chandeliers hanging from the high ceiling.

A woman identical to the one who was supposed to be his bride.

Elizabeth laughed, the hearty sound reminding him that her similarities to Sarah were only physical. Her temperament, her attitudes toward a woman's role, even her disregard for rules sharply contrasted to Sarah's.

Society's rules for women were much more relaxed in the west, though, and the thought popped into his brain that Elizabeth, being the kind of woman she was, might be happier in Colorado than she was back east.

Something inside him warmed at the sound of her laughter and he couldn't help but smile at the pure joy on her face. Elizabeth's laugh had always been infectious, and as she looked up, their eyes met for a moment before she turned back to her partner and gave him a wide smile.

Jealousy slammed into Cole's gut a fraction of a second before desire hit him even lower. Hunger swept through him, filling his veins. He wanted her.

He swore.

"What's wrong with you?" Quinn's voice cut into his thoughts as he came and leaned with his back against the bar, watching the dancing. "You're supposed to be happy, not looking like you want to tear somebody's head off. Unless you're just in a hurry to get Sarah upstairs and into your bed."

"She's not Sarah."

Quinn's head spun around to face him so fast Cole thought it might spin clear off. "What?"

"It's Bee."

Quinn didn't say a word, just turned back and

watched with wide eyes as Bee was twirled around the floor by one man after another.

"That's Bee?"

Cole nodded.

Quinn began to chuckle. The sound grew louder, his eyes watering until the deep timbre of his laugh filled Cole's ears and practically drowned out the music.

Cole glared at his brother. Nothing about this was funny.

"What happened?" Quinn asked when his laughter finally died down.

Cole explained the situation, but he couldn't come up with any reasonable explanation for why his common sense had deserted him and he'd married Bee, anyway.

"How are you planning to explain to the folks in town that she's not the woman you sent for?"

Cole shrugged. He hadn't thought that far ahead. He'd have to talk to Bee later and between the two of them, concoct a story that would even keep Mrs. Lundstrom's tongue from wagging. "I'll think of something."

Quinn nodded. "Better do it soon before they find out from your bride."

"I will."

"Well," Quinn said, his gaze following Bee as she was swept up in another dance, "being married to Bee, your life won't be dull. And whether it's Bee or Sarah, you've got yourself a mighty fine-looking woman."

Cole had to agree. From ringlets and freckles as a girl, Elizabeth had grown into a beautiful woman.

"And since it didn't take much thinking before you decided to marry her," Quinn went on, "maybe you like her a little bit more than you let on."

With another small laugh, Quinn walked off, leaving his words burning into Cole's brain.

CHAPTER 4

*E*lizabeth's gaze strayed to the far end of the hotel ballroom. Cole was leaning with his back against the polished walnut bar running the length of the room. One foot rested on a brass rail as he watched the dancers twirling around the room.

He's so handsome, she thought, a tingling sensation rushing through her. His chest and shoulders filled out the black frock coat he was wearing as if it had been specially tailored for him, and the snow-white shirt emphasized his sun-bronzed skin. A paisley cravat and diamond pin completed his outfit, and if she wasn't well aware they were in the west, she would have believed they were in one of the finest hotels in Philadelphia.

Even the town…Rocky Ridge…was more advanced than she'd expected. She'd studied everything ever written about the west, and although much of the town was quite primitive, the hotel where their wedding feast was being held was beautifully decorated.

The ballroom wasn't as large as the hotel ballrooms in the east, but what it lacked in size, it more than made up for in furnishings. Crystal chandeliers hanging from a high corniced ceiling illuminated the room wallpapered in flocked velvet. Intricately carved chairs and couches sat along the walls of the room and a richly polished fluted walnut bar ran along one end.

She rested her gaze back on Cole. Her husband. The dream she'd held in her heart for so many years had come true.

No, not the way she'd hoped, but now that they were married, she had time to show him how much she loved him, and time for him to fall in love with her.

And there was no doubt in her mind that one day, he would.

Excitement and anticipation of their future together bubbled up inside her, and she couldn't stop the smile tugging at her lips. She wished she could learn to control her emotions, she thought, but she'd never been able to hide her feelings well. Even now, she wondered if Cole knew she'd been lying about her reasons for taking Sarah's place.

Suddenly, Cole looked up and their eyes met. He seemed to be studying her, the intensity in his gaze causing a disturbing awareness flowing through her.

Many young women of her age would be ignorant of the cause, but she was well informed about the physical intimacies between men and women. She and her friend, Poppy, had learned more than they'd expected thanks to the medical texts she and her best friend had pored over one rainy afternoon while Poppy's father, Summerton's doctor, was out.

At the time, she couldn't imagine ever wanting anything more than companionship. Then she'd met Cole, and her world had changed forever.

"Welcome to Rocky Ridge, Mrs. Berringer."

Elizabeth tore her gaze away from Cole and spun around. A woman Elizabeth guessed was about the same age as her aunt stood in front of her, a smile on her round face. "Hello."

"I'm Agnes Mulgrew," the woman said. "My husband, Cy, works for Cole. We're neighbors. I can't tell you how pleased I am to finally have female company out at the ranch. It does get lonely sometimes."

"Please call me E—" Elizabeth stopped in mid-word. What was Cole going to tell everyone? Was he going to admit she wasn't the woman he'd sent for, or did he expect her to carry on the pretense indefinitely? "Bee," she corrected herself. "I'm happy to meet you."

For a few uncomfortable moments, Elizabeth wondered if she'd made a dreadful mistake. But she hadn't had time to ask Cole how they would handle introductions.

"Please, call me Agnes," the woman said, her pale blue eyes twinkling. "I hope we'll become good friends.

My, that is an unusual name," she commented. "Where did it come from?"

Elizabeth relaxed slightly. At least she wouldn't have to concoct a story about the origins of her nickname. "Oh, nothing exciting," she replied. "When we were young, Cole and his brother used to tell me I reminded them of a bee always buzzing about. They began calling me Bee and the name stuck." She leaned in a little as if she was about to impart a secret. "Of course, nicknames weren't acceptable for young ladies in Pennsylvania, but I think here I should like to be known as Bee."

Agnes chuckled, the wrinkles in her face deepening until her eyes almost disappeared into the folds of her cheeks. "Then Bee it is. I hope you and Cole will be very happy," she went on. "He's waited for this day for a long time."

Elizabeth's heart lurched with that already-familiar ache. "You know him well?" she asked.

Agnes nodded. "I love Cole and his brother like they were my own sons," she replied. "I'd hate to see either of them hurt, so I'm especially glad you came. And I hope one day soon, Quinn can find himself a wife and settle down, too."

Elizabeth was glad Cole and Quinn had someone who cared about them and wanted them to be happy. Guilt washed over her, but she tamped it down. Sarah had hurt Cole. She hadn't. She could honestly say she'd never do anything to intentionally hurt him.

"Now, I'll let you get back to your dancing. I haven't seen you dancing with your new husband yet, though," Agnes said, her eyes twinkling.

Elizabeth wanted nothing more than to dance with Cole. They'd danced together once, at her sixteenth birthday party, even though he hadn't known it at the time and as far as she knew, still had no idea he'd held her in his arms and not Sarah. Thinking she was Sarah because they were both dressed exactly alike, he'd asked if she had space on her dance card. She'd happily entered his name.

The small orchestra had played one of her favorite waltzes. He'd held her almost at arms' length, as was acceptable in society, and even though the ballroom was filled with dancers, to Elizabeth, for those few minutes, she and Cole were the only two people in the world.

At that moment, her fantasy was born. In it, Cole's arms would be around her, his heart beating against her chest as they twirled around the room. He would gaze into her eyes and she would see her love reflected in those depths. Then he'd lean close and whisper words of desire and devotion in her ear moments before he kissed her.

"Are you staying in town for a few days?"

Agnes's voice interrupted Elizabeth's musings. She felt herself blush at the direction her thoughts had gone. "No," she replied. "We'll be going to the ranch in the morning. Cole is anxious to get back, and to be honest, I'm eager to see my new home."

"Speaking of home, I do have to speak to some friends before I collect Cy and get home. He's not much for parties, so I'm surprised I've managed to keep him away from the ranch as long as I have."

"It was so nice to meet you," Elizabeth said. "If we're neighbors, I'm sure I'll see you again soon."

Elizabeth watched as Agnes moved through the crowd, pausing to speak to several people before she stopped beside Cole. He nodded at something Agnes said, then smiled at the woman as she reached up and patted his cheek affectionately.

Then he lifted his head and looked in her direction, the smile fading from his face.

Unease fluttered through Elizabeth. What had Agnes said to Cole?

Cole looked on as Bee was swept up in a reel by one of the ranch hands from the Triple M, the ranch belonging to Cade and Bella Morgan. In the pale cream-colored gown she'd changed into for their wedding and with her hair swept up away from her neck, she was a vision, and was attracting the attention of every cowboy in the room.

An unwelcome vision flashed into his mind—one of Bee in his bed, her sunlight-colored hair glistening in the faint lamplight, her eyes welcoming him, her lips swollen from his kisses.

Yet it was Bee he'd been picturing in his bed, not Sarah. Yes, the two women were identical in appearance, but he'd never seen Sarah's eyes darken with desire. He'd never been intimate with Bee either, but somehow he suspected she would be less reserved and more open to his lovemaking.

"Hell, no," he muttered, then realizing he'd spoken the words aloud, added an apology to the two people standing next to him.

"What's the matter, boss?" Cy Mulgrew, his foreman, sidled up beside him. "You sure don't look like a fella who's finally got everything he wants."

Because he wasn't, he wanted to say. He should've had everything he'd ever wanted, would've had if Sarah had been on that stage instead of Bee.

He was proud of what he'd accomplished since he'd settled in Rocky Ridge. Time and hours of back-breaking labor had turned the rundown ranch he'd bought into a small, but growing and highly respected, operation. He'd rebuilt the house and the outbuildings, and was turning a good profit.

And a few weeks ago, after he'd gone over the accounts, he'd finally felt confident that he could provide a decent and comfortable home for Sarah and their children.

He took a long draw of the amber liquid, feeling the burn as it slid down his throat. "Just thinking, Cy."

"You ain't sorry you got hitched already, are you?" Cy asked, his weathered skin creased in a frown.

"Yessir, it's a strange thing, marriage is. Even though it seems like it'll always be a bed of roses, there's always thorns along the way, and there's no way of tellin' how folks will handle 'em."

Cy nodded in agreement with himself. His stick-straight silver hair bobbed with every movement of his head.

Cole slid a glance at him. "Philosophical tonight, aren't you?"

"It's that kind of night," Cy murmured. "But I wanted to tell you one of the fences is down out at the south pasture. I'll round up a few of the men in the morning and we'll ride out there and take care of it."

"Thanks, Cy. I'd appreciate it. I'll be back at the ranch by noon, and we can talk then."

Cy leaned his back against the bar and folded his arms across his chest. With a slight jerk of his head, he gestured toward Bee. "I'd say you'd best go rescue your bride before one of those young scalawags scoops her up and carries her away."

Cole glanced in Bee's direction. She was surrounded by men, and a sudden stab of jealousy stabbed him. What the hell—? Why would he care who she was talking to?

He didn't, he assured himself, even as his stomach clenched and he had a sudden urge to both punch the men and grab her and whisk her upstairs to his bed at the same time.

Still, she was his wife now. People expected him to

be in love, and a man in love wouldn't stand by while other men ogled his wife.

The music stopped, and the cowpuncher Bee had been dancing with ushered her back toward the far corner of the room. Again, jealousy speared him, even though he couldn't for the life of him figure out why. He straightened and set his empty glass on the bar. "You go enjoy yourself, Cy. I'm going to get my bride."

Straightening, he left Cy behind and strode across the ballroom to where Bee was surrounded by men. She was laughing again, and it struck him that she'd always laughed a lot more than Sarah had.

Sarah had always been the more serious of the two girls growing up, cautious, concerned with appearances and propriety. Bee, on the other hand, had always been a bit wild, with a need to experience life first-hand, always ready for any hairbrained scheme he or Quinn had thought up.

A smile tugged at his lips as memories rushed through his brain—Bee sneaking out to go swimming in the pond behind the grain mill, riding astride whenever no one was looking, arm wrestling with Horace Schumacher at a birthday party.

He stopped beside Bee and cupped her elbow. Even through the fabric, her heat snaked through him and settled low in his belly. An uncomfortable sensation he didn't want to admit to filled him.

Bee looked up at him. Her gaze bored into him, and

a tiny frown marred her perfect forehead. Had she felt it, too?

"May I have the next dance?" he asked, surprised at the shakiness in his voice.

"I…" She gazed at him for a few moments before a slow smile lifted her lips. "I'd like that."

The music started up again, a waltz this time. He ushered her into the center of the room. His chest tightened. It should be Sarah in his arms, not Bee. So why did holding Bee feel so good, so natural?

Bee looked up at him. "Are you all right?" she asked. "You never really liked dancing, if I remember correctly. You told me that the last time we danced—"

"We've never danced together before," he put in.

A slight flush brightened her cheeks. "Oh…yes… that's right. My mistake. I must have been thinking about someone else."

Something in the tone of her voice niggled at him. He didn't quite believe her, but why, he couldn't say. Surely he would remember if he'd ever danced with her. Wouldn't he?

Not soon enough, the music faded. "I think we should go," he said. "I want to get an early start in the morning and we have some things we need to talk about."

"Whatever you say," she told him, turning away and heading toward a group of guests standing near the ballroom entrance.

A half hour later, he was following Bee up the stairs

to their room. It had taken a lot longer than he'd expected to say their goodnights, and there had been a few times he'd been sure Bee was about to say something, but she'd quickly corrected herself.

But finally, they'd made their escape, and as they walked together down the corridor toward their room, he couldn't help wondering how he was supposed to handle their wedding night.

CHAPTER 5

"What will we do now?" Elizabeth stood just inside the doorway of their hotel room. No, she amended. Not their wedding night. His and Sarah's.

The room was smaller than her bedroom back east. A bureau with a jug and basin sat against one wall, and a wardrobe on another. There was a chair and a round table near the window looking out to the street below. A heavy iron bed covered with a wedding-ring quilt that seemed to fill the room.

Her face heated. The photos and text in the medical books hadn't prepared her for the reality of what men and women did together in the marriage bed.

At the same time, she couldn't prevent the sparks of anticipation and excitement coursing through her.

Cole had obviously been devastated at her confession that she wasn't Sarah, yet a few minutes later, he'd taken her to the church and made her his wife. She'd had a few anxious moments when she'd signed their marriage license, but since her middle name was Susan, she'd signed Elizabeth S. Main, and explained that everyone used her middle name. She'd said a silent prayer that God wouldn't strike her down for embellishing the truth in His house, and she'd been relieved when the preacher had accepted her explanation without question.

Before the ceremony, Cole had told her why he was going to marry her. There were no feelings involved. He wanted a wife and eventually a family. Nothing more.

Since he couldn't have Sarah, she'd do. It was less than flattering to be bluntly told that she was second best, and she'd have to live the rest of her life knowing that she was a substitute for the woman he really loved.

Was it enough that he was her husband now, no matter the reason? Surely if she loved him enough, in time he'd forget about Sarah and he'd fall in love with her. Then they could have the life she dreamed of.

"First," Cole said as he set his hat on the bureau, "we need to figure out what people are going to call you."

"I thought of that," she replied. "I introduced myself as Bee."

His brows arched. "Why did you do that?"

"I assumed you'd prefer that I didn't announce to everyone that I'm not the woman you planned to marry."

"Well, no, I didn't plan to tell anyone, but—"

"They accepted it once I explained it was a nickname."

He gazed at her for what seemed an eternity, his eyes dark, the muscle in his jaw pulsing. Finally, he nodded. "That was smart."

"You and Quinn have called me Bee for years. There's not much chance you'll slip and call me Elizabeth."

"That's true."

"So there's no reason anyone should ever know the truth unless you choose to tell them."

Cole perched on the side of the bed and tugged off his boots. "Quinn knows."

"You told him?"

His eyes darkened. "I needed to talk to somebody, and who else would understand more than my brother?"

Elizabeth considered that for a few moments. She had put him in a difficult situation, and she regretted it. If the tables were turned, she would have confided in Sarah. "What did he say?"

Cole nodded, and a slight smile tilted his lips. "I think he's looking forward to seeing how we deal with it. He finds the whole thing amusing."

"It's not amusing at all. Marriage is serious, not to be taken lightly."

"You know Quinn never takes anything seriously."

She nodded. "I'd forgotten how dead set against

marriage he was. Now that I think about it, I'm sure he would find this whole situation entertaining."

"He won't mention it in your presence, so it's not something to concern yourself with." He yawned. "I think we should go to bed now."

Awareness spread through her at the thought that he might expect her to lie with him. She'd heard the act was unpleasant, but she couldn't imagine Cole ever hurting her or being unkind.

In fact, her skin tingled in anticipation, and her heart raced in her chest.

"You don't have to worry," he said. "I'm not going to exercise my rights, but I am going to sleep in the bed. We're married so there's no reason not to, but the chair's available if you aren't comfortable with that."

Relief and disappointment waged a war inside her. She could admit she'd been worried about what the night would bring, while at the same time, she'd been eager to learn the secrets of the marriage bed, especially with the man she loved. But Cole didn't love her, didn't care about her at all, so she shouldn't be surprised he had no interest in her, physically or otherwise. "Of course, there's no reason we can't share the bed since we are husband and wife," she said, noticing the threadiness in her voice. "I appreciate that you're not going to take advantage of me."

He looked at her, his gaze intense as it slid from her head to the tips of her toes. "Trust me, Bee, if I ever made love to you, you would not feel taken advantage of."

She felt her face flame. Her voice stuck in her throat and her heart pounded so hard she was afraid she might break a rib. She spun around so he couldn't see how his words were affecting her.

As slowly as she could manage to give herself a few moments to get her emotions under control, she put her hat and reticule on the bureau.

By the time she felt her body return to normal and she turned around, he'd taken off his shirt and pants and was standing before her dressed only in undergarments. Her breath made a loud sound when she sucked in a gasp.

She'd never seen a male chest before, and the sight of his muscles rippling beneath his tanned skin sent shivers of heat deep into her core. She wanted nothing more at that moment than to touch him, to feel the movement of those muscles beneath her fingers.

Shocked by her wanton thoughts, she found herself speechless for the first time in her life.

"Do you need me to help you get out of that gown?" he asked, taking a few steps toward her.

Never before had she felt such…she couldn't even describe the sensations racing through her. The thought of him touching her…"No!"

"You can manage all those buttons down the back by yourself?" he asked, his lips quirked in an amused grin.

He knew she couldn't, and it infuriated her that she'd put herself in a position where she needed to accept his help. Of course, when she'd chosen the gown for today, she hadn't expected to confess to the trick she'd planned to play on him.

She'd expected him to help her unbutton the gown, to revel in his touch, to finally be able to show him how much she loved him.

Now, she'd have to suffer through his hands on her in silence. "No, I suppose I can't."

"Where are your nightclothes?" he asked.

"In my valise." Her valise was piled in the corner of the room, apparently taken there by someone during the ceremony. She opened it and drew out a white silk nightgown.

"Turn around," he ordered once she had draped the nightgown on the bed.

She did as he ordered, her teeth clenched as his fingers worked the buttons, his warm hands grazing her skin on her back as the gown parted and finally fell to the floor in a puddle, leaving her standing in her chemise and corset.

He tugged on the laces of her corset, and she felt it loosen a moment before she heard his footsteps move away.

"Turn the light out when you're done," he said, then slid into the bed, turned away from her and pulled the sheet and quilt over him. "Goodnight."

The morning dawned crisp and clear. Elizabeth breathed in the fresh mountain air as Cole and Quinn prepared to take her toward the ranch that would be her new home.

Cole helped her into the wagon, then climbed up beside her.

She'd barely slept the night before, but she'd never felt more alert and alive than at that moment. Her new life was about to begin. It had been a little uncomfortable when she'd had to face Quinn over breakfast in the hotel dining room that morning, but he hadn't made any comments about what Cole had told him, and her estimation of him had risen a few notches at his kindness.

"Are you cold?" Cole asked. "I can get the blanket in the back for you if you need it."

The air was cool, but invigorating. She shook her head.

"So we're ready?" Cole picked up the reins.

"What about Quinn?" Elizabeth asked, twisting to look behind her, searching for Quinn.

"We don't have to wait for him. He has his own horse." Cole flicked the reins. The sudden movement when the horses moved jostled Elizabeth and sent her sideways into Cole.

Quickly, she scrambled away, gripping the metal handle beside the seat so she wouldn't lose her balance again as the wagon rolled over the dried ruts in the road.

Just then, Quinn rode up beside them, slowing his pace to match theirs.

As they left Rocky Ridge behind, the two men kept the conversation light, pointing out the various landmarks they passed, commenting on the weather, the landscape and the wildlife they came across on the way.

Elizabeth took it all in, falling in love with her new home more and more with every passing minute. She'd never felt as if she really fit in when she lived in the city, and now, she was sure this wild country was where she truly belonged.

After a while, Quinn rode off after promising to be back for supper.

The trail curved and climbed until it flattened out before it dipped into a shallow valley. Cole drew the wagon to a halt. His face took on a contented expression as he gazed out over the vast expanse in front of them. "There it is, Bee," he said.

She heard the pride in his voice and noticed his lips curve in a smile.

Ahead of her was undisturbed land as far as she could see. In the distance, foothills gradually rose from the valley and transformed into snow-tipped mountains reaching to the sky.

Hundreds of cows dotted the empty land, and a river flowed nearby, the water sparkling in the sunshine.

She shifted to face him. "This is all yours?"

"Sort of," he replied. "See the two houses over there?"

Elizabeth's gaze followed Cole's outstretched finger pointing to a small group of buildings. "One's mine. One belongs to Quinn. The boundary line between my ranch and Quinn's runs between the houses. We decided to build the houses near each other. That way we're close enough to help each other when we need it, and we figured that when the time came we both got married and raised a family, there'd be company for our wives and children."

"Quinn's married?"

Cole chuckled. "No. He hasn't even thought about settling down yet."

"You mean no woman yet has held his attention for more than an evening or two?"

Cole seemed to consider the question for a few moments, then shook his head. "Can't think of one."

"One day the right woman will come along," she said. "I'm sure of it."

"I hope so, for your sake." Cole clicked the reins and the horses began to move. "It's a pretty lonely life out here. You're going to miss having friends close by."

Elizabeth had thought of that many times during the trip. Yes, she'd miss her friends. She'd admit that. But she'd have the one thing she'd always wanted—to be Cole's wife.

And she was sure she'd make new friends here in Rocky Ridge. "What about Agnes?" she asked. "She said she's a neighbor."

Cole laughed. "Sorry, Bee. A neighbor here can be

more than a mile away. Cy and Agnes live over that ridge.”

“Oh.” She was disappointed. She’d been looking forward to having some female companionship nearby, but she wouldn’t let anything spoil her mood. “It’ll be fine, Cole. I’m sure I won’t have time for socializing, anyway. I’ll be busy looking after the house and helping you with your work around the ranch.” And our children, she wanted to add, but bit her tongue to prevent the words from slipping out. If the night before was any indication, he had no intention of making theirs a real marriage, and without that, there would be no children.

Hopefully, one day, he’d love her as much as she loved him, and things would change. In the meantime, she’d be content and try to be happy with whatever he was willing to give.

“Oh, Cole,” she murmured, entranced. “It’s…absolutely stunning. All of it.”

He looked over at her and studied her face. Then he grinned, as if he was satisfied she was telling the truth and not offering up an empty compliment. “I’m glad you like it.”

“I do,” she repeated, excitement bubbling through her. “Now hurry. I want to see my new home.”

Cole watched Bee’s bright smile fade when he opened the front door of the house a half hour later. And he knew why.

Dust covered the heavy furniture. Books and papers were strewn about on every surface. Dried mud caked the floors. And that was only in the main room. The kitchen and the bedroom were even worse.

"I'm sorry," he said. And he was. "I should have warned you. I had a housekeeper, and I expected her to stay once you…I mean, Sarah…arrived. But after I wrote the letter, she decided to go back east to live with her family. I couldn't find another one, at least not one that didn't want more than a job. And since I couldn't work the ranch and look after the house, I had to choose. There was only one choice I could make."

Elizabeth nodded absently. "Of course. I understand that. I just wasn't prepared…" She brightened. "I'll have this all cleaned up as soon as possible."

"You've never done housework," he pointed out.

"No, I haven't, but I paid very close attention to the housekeeper when she cleaned and did laundry, so I'm sure I can handle it."

"And I'll bet you've never cooked a meal, have you?"

She grinned. "You would have lost your money. Mrs. Doughty let me help her when Aunt Meg was out. I'm actually a very good cook."

Cole's brows lifted. "You can cook? And you're going to scrub my dirty clothes and clean the house?"

"I expected to take care of you and your home," she said.

"I'll get another housekeeper as soon as I can—"

"There's no need." She gazed up at him. It shocked him that she'd prepared to be a wife, to take care of the domestic responsibilities of marriage.

Her smile disappeared. "Not unless you don't want me to…"

They'd been friends growing up, and she'd never once given him any sign that she'd ever marry a man who didn't have a housekeeper and a cook. "I didn't think you'd ever want to be domestic."

"There's a lot about me you don't know, Cole."

"Looks like it," he murmured. What other surprises did she have in store for him?

Her smile returned. "Do you remember Mrs. Doughty?"

"I do."

"She was so possessive about her recipes, and I knew she would never share them willingly. But once I made my decision to come west, I sneaked into the kitchen late at night and copied the recipes I already knew how to make as well as few I wanted to try. It was stealing in a way, and I do regret it. I'll write and confess to Mrs. Doughty as soon as I get settled."

He wasn't surprised at the way she'd prepared for her trip west. She'd always been impulsive, but once she did set her mind on something, nothing stopped her, and she'd do whatever she had to do to make it happen, even bending the rules whenever she thought it was necessary.

"I don't have time to show you around," he said. "Being away yesterday and this morning means chores got behind. There are four bedrooms. Pick one for yourself and I'll take your trunk and valise up tonight. There's a slab of beef in the cold cellar. We'll be back for supper at six."

Before she could respond, he spun around and left, letting the door slam behind him.

For several long moments, Elizabeth stood at the door taking in the disaster that was now her home. Shaking her head in disbelief at the state of the room, she wandered through the parlor to the dining room. A large oak table that would sit twelve comfortably filled the center of the room. Dishes and silverware filled a large oak sideboard and hutch set against the wall near a large window.

She let out a gasp of horror when she stepped into the kitchen. Dirty dishes and pots covered the worktable and the dry sink. Even the cookstove was littered with dishes and dried-on food.

Four hours, she muttered. It would take every minute of that time to clean up the mess and try to find food to feed Cole and…who? He'd said *they'd* be back for supper. Who were *they?* How many men was she expected to cook for?

Well, she decided, better make enough for a dozen. If there were leftovers, they could eat them the next day.

A closed door in the kitchen drew her attention. Opening it, she saw it led to a cold cellar. The shelves were well-stocked with all the staples she'd need to prepare a meal. After a quick search, she found the beef roast he expected her to cook as well as onions, carrots, potatoes and a few apples that were starting to shrivel but were still usable.

Piling the supplies she'd need in her arms, she took them into the kitchen, then realizing there wasn't anywhere to put them, took them back into the cold cellar and set them all in an empty space on one of the shelves. Then she lit the stove so it could heat while she worked on the mountain of dirty dishes. A half hour later, she'd scrubbed and dried enough pots and utensils to get the roast started. She placed the meat in the bottom of a large pan. After she'd peeled and chopped the vegetables, she arranged them around the roast, adding a sprinkle of spices before she slid the pan into the oven. Then she whipped up some dough for rolls and set them to rise before turning her attention back to cleaning.

For the next three hours, she worked until every dish in the kitchen was washed, dried and put away. She scoured the worktable and even scrubbed the floor until she was satisfied it was as clean as she could possibly make it.

She checked the roast, pleased that it was cooking perfectly. She glanced at the grandfather clock in the parlor. She had time to make dessert, too. She was just putting the finishing touches to an apple cobbler when she heard the front door open.

CHAPTER 6

*P*eeking around the doorway to the kitchen, Elizabeth saw Cole come inside, followed by three men she didn't recognize.

Her cheeks were flushed from the heat coming off the stove, and her hair had slipped from the tight knot at her nape. She'd hoped to have time to at least make herself more presentable before Cole came home, but it had taken her longer than she'd hoped to get the meal prepared.

"I hope whatever your new missus is cooking tastes as good as it smells," a man with gray hair that reminded Elizabeth of bristles on a broom said to Cole.

She ducked back into the kitchen before they saw her.

"Me, too," she heard Cole say. "It looks like we might be having company for supper, too. I haven't seen a table set this nice since I left home."

Elizabeth grinned. They weren't having company, but she'd set the table with the best china and silverware she could find, and she'd even gone out and picked a few wildflowers to use as a centerpiece.

Slipping her apron off over her head, she tucked her hair behind her ears and smoothed her butter yellow dress before she went into the parlor where the men were hanging up their hats on the hook behind the door.

"You're all right on time. Supper's ready," she said. "Please sit down and I'll bring it through."

"Who else is coming?" Cole asked.

"No one. You didn't tell me how many to expect for supper, so since the table seats twelve, I prepared for a full house."

"You're right. I didn't. I'm sorry. I shouldn't have rushed out the way I did. It'll usually be the five of us at noon, but only you and me for supper unless you invite somebody."

She only counted four. "Five?"

"Quinn is usually here, but he's eating supper in town tonight. Now, let me introduce you to the men. They work harder than any men I know and I couldn't run this ranch without them. They usually eat supper in the bunkhouse but they wanted to meet you, so I invited them to eat with us tonight. I hope you don't mind."

"That's fine, Cole. There's plenty of food."

Elizabeth smiled at the three men taking off their hats.

"This here is Cy Mulgrew," Cole said, indicating the

man with the sparse gray hair and sun-darkened skin on his right.

"How do, ma'am," Cy said, nodding.

The tall, lean man with a twinkle in his eyes on Cole's left took a step forward. "Pete Voss, ma'am," he said. "Pleased to make your acquaintance."

"And this is TJ," Cole put in, jerking his head in the direction of a fair-haired, freckled man who seemed little more than a boy.

"Howdy, ma'am."

Elizabeth shook each man's hand. "Please, call me Bee. I'm happy to meet you all. Please come in and sit down before the food gets cold."

The men hurried into the dining room and took their seats. Elizabeth was aware of Cole's eyes following her as she flitted around the room, carrying more platters and bowls filled with vegetables and freshly baked rolls.

Finally, she paused, glancing from one chair to the other as if she wasn't sure where she should sit.

"Are you ready to join us?" Cole asked. The men stood and Cole pulled out the empty chair beside him. "Sit here," he said. "The boys left it for you."

She smiled softly and hurried to take her place.

After a short blessing, the only sounds in the room where those of cutlery scraping against plates as the bowls were passed around and the men filled their plates.

During the meal, Elizabeth listened to the conversation as they discussed the various chores around the ranch, the new calves that had been born that spring, and their plans for the roundup and trail drive to Denver a few months away.

"That was a mighty fine meal, Bee," Cole said when he'd finished his second helping of apple cobbler. He wiped his mouth with the napkin and leaned back in his chair. "Best I've had since I got here."

The other four men echoed Cole's words, praising her cooking skills and commenting that if she kept cooking like that, they'd be so fat they wouldn't be able to climb up into their saddles without the horses collapsing under them.

"Thank you." Bee's voice was barely more than a whisper. Heat rose in her cheeks and she lowered her gaze so Cole couldn't see the joy she was trying to hide.

She was thrilled he liked her cooking. She'd always heard the way to a man's heart was through his stomach, which was one of the reasons she'd made a point of learning to cook.

It was a start.

The men were gone, and for the first time, Cole and Bee were alone in the house where they'd live until they died. He sat at the table, his eyes following her as she cleared the dirty dishes and put them into a basin of hot water.

He studied her while she worked. A soft smile

played on her lips. What was she thinking? He'd never known any woman to enjoy scrubbing dishes.

It occurred to him he didn't even know her anymore. She really was a mystery to him, and one he'd have to solve since she was his wife now.

She'd been embarrassed by the men's compliments on her cooking. But why? He'd never seen that side of her before. Growing up, she'd always been full of confidence, facing everything and everybody head on. She'd always been the first one to agree to any outing or adventure any of them thought up. Now, a few kind words made her blush.

He had to admit the change intrigued him. She wasn't the same woman he'd left six years before, and he found he wanted to get to know the new Bee. It annoyed and excited him at the same time. He only hoped she hadn't changed too much. He'd liked the old Bee.

And he was attracted to her. When she'd come out of the kitchen before supper with her cheeks pink and her hair loose from the tight bun at her neck, desire had hit him. Hard. And then she'd smiled at him, and suddenly, he'd had a vision of what she might look like after a night in his bed, all flushed and her hair like a cloud against the pillow.

He tried to tell himself his physical reaction to her was only because she was the spitting image of Sarah. Still, deep down he knew there was something else. Something more.

"I wish there was something I could do to help with the chores," Bee said as she set the last plate back on the shelf. "There seems to be so much work to do that I'd be happy to—"

Her words interrupted his thoughts, and when he met her gaze, the expression on her face made him wonder if she'd seen through him. "You don't need to concern yourself," he told her. "Your job is to look after the house."

Her smile disappeared and her lips pursed. Cole realized he'd just made a huge mistake. "My job? Is that why you decided to go ahead with the marriage? Because you needed a housekeeper?"

He couldn't answer, because he honestly still didn't know why he'd decided to marry her. He hadn't been thinking, and he'd lost his senses, but he was pretty sure he shouldn't tell her that. "I didn't mean it that way. I only meant that you don't have to be concerned about the ranch."

Bee folded the dish towel, focusing on making the edges precise before she set it on the counter. Then she looked up at him and took a step toward him. "This is my home now. All of it, and I'm interested in everything about it. I want to know how the ranch works, what kinds of chores there are every day, what you do with the cows—"

"Cattle."

"What?"

He grinned. "They're cattle, not cows."

"Oh." Her anger faded and she laughed. That was one of the things he'd always liked about her. She could be furious, but once she'd made her point, she didn't hold a grudge. Her anger didn't last long before she was back to her cheerful self.

He liked the sound of her laughter. It wasn't a feminine twitter like some women's giggles, but filled the room.

"Well, then, I want to know about your *cattle* and horses, and everything else."

"It's not something most women care about."

Her brows lifted and she met his gaze squarely. "You've known me for years. Do you really think I'm like most women?"

He looked down at her, his chest tightening with a strange sensation he didn't recognize. No, she wasn't like most women. In fact, he'd never met another woman quite like her. And he didn't want to like it one bit.

He stepped away, crossing to the door. "It's late. Time to turn in. Did you decide what room you want? I'll take your trunk upstairs for you."

She didn't answer for a few seconds, and he wondered if she was waiting for a response to her question. Thankfully, she let the subject drop. "The room beside yours," she said. "The view from the window is spectacular."

It was, which was why, when he'd built the house, he'd built a balcony onto his room looking out over the ranch to the mountains in the distance. The room Bee had chosen had the same view, with a door that opened to the same balcony.

A few minutes later, they climbed the stairs. Bee paused in the doorway to her bedroom and turned back as he opened his door. She gazed up at him, and his chest tightened at the regret in her eyes. "I know I'm not the woman you wanted, but I promise I will be a good wife to you."

The words speared him. She'd told him she'd come west was because she wanted adventure. But there would be no adventure, only hard work. Yet she seemed content with that.

He had a sudden urge to take her into his arms and kiss her senseless. He even took a step toward her before his good sense stopped him. He didn't love her. He was in love with Sarah. It was only because she was identical to the woman he loved and he'd lost that these urges were haunting him.

It had nothing to do with Bee, he repeated to himself as she gazed at him, confusion in her eyes.

"Goodnight, Bee." He stepped into his room and closed his door behind him. As he undressed and slid between the sheets, her words echoed in his brain.

She'd lied about why she'd left home and come to Colorado. He was sure of it. He had no reason for thinking the way he did, only that his gut was telling him there was more to her reasons for coming west than she'd let on. The question was, what were they?

Elizabeth yawned and stretched, forgetting for a moment that she wasn't back in her bed in Summerton. Then she remembered, and a smile tugged at her mouth.

She'd opened the window a little the night before, and now the air was chilly, but she didn't care. She bounded out of bed and hurried to the window. The morning sun glistened off the snow still covering the mountain peaks. The scent of cedar met her nose.

This was the beginning of her new life as Cole's wife, and she couldn't wait to get started. She was annoyed with herself that she'd slept so late. She'd planned to be up before dawn, but her fatigue from her long journey west had caught up with her.

After a quick wash, she ran a brush through her hair and pinned it back. Then she slipped into a dress she'd hung up the night before and hurried downstairs.

She hoped to find Cole in the kitchen since his bedroom door had been open when she'd come out of her room, but both the kitchen and the parlor were empty.

The stove had been lit and a basket of eggs sat on the table, so she assumed he hadn't gone far and would be in for breakfast soon. She wasn't sure if the other men would be joining them as well, so she decided to prepare for that possibility.

She scooped coffee grounds into the coffeepot and set it on the stove to brew while she prepared the rest of the meal.

She remembered seeing a slab of bacon the day before, so she quickly retrieved it and sliced it up, setting it to cook while she whipped up a batch of scrambled eggs. Bread, butter and preserves rounded out the meal.

She was slicing the bread when Cole came in and strolled into the kitchen. He was alone. His brows lifted when he saw the amount of food on the table.

"You didn't say how many men I'd have to feed for breakfast."

Looking around, he grinned and nodded. "I'm sorry. I forgot to tell you it's just us for breakfast," he said. "You made enough food to keep us going for the next two days since the boys don't eat with us in the mornings."

"That's not a bad thing," Elizabeth replied. "I have

enough work to keep me busy. I won't have to spend the time cooking breakfast every day."

"I didn't expect breakfast today. You slept late. I wondered if you were going to sleep the day away."

He was smiling, and she recognized the teasing glint in his eyes. At the same time, Elizabeth already felt guilty about oversleeping, but he had no idea what she'd gone through to get here. "It's been an exhausting journey and I was tired—"

Cole bounded out of the chair and crossed to where she was standing near the stove. "I was teasing," he said, hooking his finger under her chin and forcing her to look up at him. "I can't believe you think I'm annoyed that you slept past dawn."

Her breathing quickened at his nearness, and his eyes boring into hers sent shivers through her. "Well… not really…but I—"

"You know me better than that, Bee."

Did she? She'd changed in the years he'd been gone. It only made sense that he'd changed, too. He was a man now, not a boy. He'd lived through a war and had had experiences that must have changed him.

"I'm not angry at all and I'm sorry if I gave you the wrong impression. It's been a long time, and we need to get to know each other again. I shouldn't expect you to remember everything about me since we didn't spend that much time together before I left."

We've spent more time together than you know, she

almost said, but clamped her lips shut in case the words came out. And during those times, she'd memorized every detail about him, from the way his hair curled at the nape of his neck when it got too long to the tiny scar on his ring finger he'd gotten the day they'd gone fishing at the pond and he'd gotten a fish hook caught in it. "You're right, and I'm sure I'm being overly sensitive."

"At least one thing hasn't changed," he said, laughter in his voice. "You still stand up for yourself." The sound was so infectious that she had no choice but to join him.

"Now," he said, holding out a chair for her, "come and eat before the food is cold, and tell me what you have planned for today."

Cole took a long drink of water from the canteen, then wiped the sweat off his forehead with his sleeve. It was unusually warm for this time of year, but he couldn't put off mending the fences. He had Quinn to help him, and he'd sent Cy and a few men to round up any strays who happened to wander off. TJ was back at the ranch keeping an eye on Tulip, one of the mares who was about to give birth.

Cole was well aware that his decision to leave TJ to look after the mare was an excuse to keep somebody close to Bee in case she needed something. He was pretty sure TJ knew it, too.

Why he was so concerned, he couldn't say. After all, Bee was a ranch wife now. She'd have to get used to being alone during the day. He couldn't afford to have one of his hands at her beck and call forever.

And Agnes was close enough if she really needed somebody.

Still, it made him uneasy to think of her being alone, for the first few days at least.

And he hadn't wanted to be the one to stay behind. He'd discovered the night before that the further he could stay away from her, the better off he'd be.

"I didn't get a chance to ask you yesterday," Quinn said. A wide grin curved his lips.

Their wedding night. That night in the hotel. A night of torture, he thought. He'd lain awake most of the night listening to Bee's soft breathing as she slept, feeling her warmth beside him, wanting…her! Not Sarah!

Guilt gnawed at him for his traitorous thoughts, but at the same time, he knew he had nothing to feel guilty about. Sarah had refused him. He owed her no loyalty now.

But as much as he wanted to put Sarah out of his mind and move on, the truth of the matter was that he loved her. Always had. Always would.

And just when he'd managed to relax enough to doze off, Bee had shifted and snuggled up next to him. Her nightgown had ridden up and her bare leg rested against his. It had taken every ounce of willpower he could muster not to wrap his arms around her and forget about the promise he'd made to her earlier. He wouldn't make love to Bee when his heart belonged to her twin.

"Well?" Quinn's voice burst into Cole's thoughts. "That good or that bad?"

Cole and Quinn hadn't had a private moment together since their talk right after the wedding. "There was no wedding night."

Quinn's brows lifted. "Why not?"

"Because I love Sarah."

"You sure? Or are you stuck in the past?"

Cole glared at his brother. "Of course I'm sure. You think I would have waited all these years if I didn't love her?"

Quinn shrugged. "You might have thought you loved her, but did you like her?"

"What?" Cole picked up the shovel and slammed it into the dirt.

"You and Sarah were never real friends like you and Bee. Did you two really have anything in common with each other?"

"What do you know about relationships?" Cole asked. "You've never stayed with one woman long enough to even know her favorite color."

"That's true," Quinn admitted. "And when I do meet a woman that I'm interested in enough to find out her favorite color, I'll make sure she's a woman I can tell my deepest secrets to, a woman I can laugh with. And more than anything else, a woman who I can call my friend. Did you have that with Sarah?"

Cole didn't answer. He couldn't, because he had no answer.

And that bothered him. He'd have to think about Quinn's question later, when he was alone.

"Seems to me you're better off being married to a friend than just somebody you want to bed," Quinn commented as he raised the hammer and pounded a nail into the fence post.

"I didn't want to just bed Sarah," Cole protested. "I expected to spend my life with her, and I thought she felt the same way."

He didn't appreciate Quinn bringing up the past. It was over and done with.

"So you still haven't—"

"No!"

"You're married to Bee now." Quinn reminded him, as if he could forget that fact. "You planning to be a monk for the rest of your life? Not have a family to carry on once you're gone?"

Why did Quinn keep asking questions he had no answers for?

"You're going to be married to Bee for a long time," Quinn went on, "and we both know you're not going to go visit the saloon. So what are you going to do?"

"I don't know." The night before, he'd wanted to follow Bee into her room and make love to her, to make their marriage real in every way.

Why did she have to pick the room right beside his anyway? He'd stared at the wall between them for hours the night before, knowing Bee was on the other side, trying to convince himself that the desire that seemed to plague him now was only because Bee looked like Sarah.

Deep down he knew it wasn't true. He hadn't been thinking about Sarah at all.

Cole seemed distracted when he came in that night for supper. Whenever Elizabeth happened to look in his direction, she caught him staring at her. He'd immediately look away, but not before she saw something in his eyes she'd never noticed before. Something she couldn't define, but that made her body tingle and her heart race.

"What's this?" he asked, crossing the kitchen and lifting the lid off the cast-iron pot on the stove.

Elizabeth had sliced the leftover beef from the night before and layered it with potatoes and onions and let it simmer on the stove while she scrubbed the parlor floor and beat the rug on the clothesline outside that afternoon. "I don't know the proper name for it, but my mother called it stovies. She often made it on washdays since she wouldn't have much time to spend in the kitchen. If you wouldn't mind carrying it to the table, I'll get the biscuits."

"You must miss your mother," he commented.

"I miss my mother and my father," she replied, sadness washing over her as it always did when she thought of her parents. "More than I can ever say." Since that terrible day when they'd been taken from her, she'd never been the same. "Sarah and I were fortunate that Aunt Meg offered us a home, and we wanted for nothing. We had clothes, jewelry, everything we could ever want. But I would have given it all up to have my parents back again."

"I understand, and I'm sorry I brought it up."

"It's all right, but can we change the subject? Tell me what you did today."

She listened intently as he told her about his day, asking questions about the things she didn't understand.

"There's a barn raising this weekend at the Patterson spread," he told her when he finished eating. "If you'd like to go with me, you can meet some of the women and start making friends."

Elizabeth had heard of barn raisings, where men came together and built a barn for someone who'd lost theirs. "What happened to their barn?"

"It was hit by lightning during a storm last week and burned to the ground."

"Oh, that's terrible…"

"Luckily none of the animals were hurt or killed, but the hay and tools that were stored in the barn were destroyed. We've got some spare supplies we're not using, so I'm going to donate them."

"That's very generous." She rose to go back into the kitchen to take the bread pudding she'd made out of the oven.

"That's what neighbors do out here."

"I'm beginning to see that."

"So, would you like to go with me?"

She set the steaming baking dish on top of a folded towel on the table. "I'd love to," she answered with a smile. "What can I do to help?"

He grinned. "Food. And lots of it. The men work up quite an appetite."

"I'd be happy to prepare something," she said as she spooned the pudding into two bowls. "How much should I make?"

Cole's hand brushed against hers as he took his bowl from her.

Her breath hitched, and her eyes widened at the sudden heat snaking up her arm.

He raised his eyes to meet hers. What thoughts were running through his mind? "As much as you have time for," he said finally.

"If you don't mind me using the wagon, I'll go into town and get more supplies. Is there anything in particular you think I should make?"

"Doesn't matter. It'll get eaten. Not lady food, though. Meat. Potatoes. Bread. Dessert." He took a spoonful of pudding and let out a sound of satisfaction. "This is really good, Bee."

"Thank you," she replied, that familiar flush creeping into her cheeks. "Using up the leftover rolls from last night. There's no reason to waste food when it's not necessary."

Cole laughed. "Frugal, too. From what Cy tells me, being frugal is one of the qualities of a perfect wife."

Elizabeth spun around and hurried into the kitchen, busying herself stacking the dirty dishes near the wash basin.

A perfect wife? She might never be perfect, but she could be the perfect wife for Cole, if only he could let himself forget Sarah.

Elizabeth had never driven a wagon before, but she was confident she could manage. It wasn't much different from riding a horse, except that she couldn't feel the horse's movements beneath her.

The ride into town was pleasant, and as long as she followed the trail, she knew she wouldn't get lost. It was strange that the trip didn't seem to take as long as the ride out to the ranch had.

Sooner than she expected, Rocky Ridge came into view, and a short time later, she pulled the wagon to a stop in front of the mercantile and set the brake before she climbed down. As she brushed a few specks of dust off her dark blue skirt, her gaze swept the street. It was busy, people hurrying about, children playing, a group of women chatting near the dressmaker's shop.

She couldn't wait to get to know people and become part of the community. She made a mental note to ask Cole if he'd mind her becoming involved in some of the ladies' activities in town. Smiling, she hurried up the stairs and went inside.

The young woman behind the counter looked up from a ledger she was writing in. "Good morning, Mrs. Berringer," she called out, smiling "It's nice to see you again."

Elizabeth approached the counter and returned the woman's smile. "Good morning. Cammie, isn't it?"

Cammie leaned forward. "Officially it's Camelia, but really, who wants to be called a flowery name like that?"

"I think it's lovely, but if you prefer to be called Cammie, then Cammie it is. And please, call me Bee."

"I do prefer Cammie," Cammie replied. "Now, how are you settling in? Do you like living on the ranch?"

"I love the ranch, and I'm settling in just fine."

"That's good news. So many women come here and before you know it, they turn around and go back east. I'm glad to hear you're not one of them. Now, what can I do for you this morning?"

"There's a barn raising this weekend."

"I know. Almost everyone I know is going." She grinned. "Including me."

Elizabeth was happy to hear that she'd know at least one person there.

"I offered to prepare some food. I've made a list." Elizabeth drew a piece of paper out of her reticule and handed it to Cammie.

Cammie's eyes widened. "You're going to cook all that?"

"I've never been to a barn raising before, and Cole told me the men need a lot of food. Is it too much?"

Cammie laughed. "He's right. There's never too much food at a barn raising. What doesn't get eaten, you take back home and eat."

"Do you have enough stock to fill my order?"

"Sure do. It'll take me a few minutes to get it together, though. Do you have any other errands to do?"

Elizabeth shook her head. "Not really, but I would like to go for a walk and see the town. I didn't have a chance to see it the day I arrived."

"Take your time," Cammie said. "I'll have everything packaged up and ready for you by the time you get back."

For the next half hour, Elizabeth strolled down the boardwalk from one end of the town to the other. Shops and businesses much like back east lined the street. They were smaller, with less selection, but certainly adequate. She was pleased to see there was a schoolhouse, too, for the time she and Cole had children.

It was too soon to think about that yet, though, she mused. But one day…

Realizing how long she'd been gone, she hurried back to the mercantile. She had to get home and get started on supper.

As Cammie had promised, her order was packed up and waiting for her. While Cammie's father, Elias, loaded the supplies in the wagon, Elizabeth stopped to chat with Cammie again. "Is there a ladies society in town?"

Cammie shook her head. "Do you knit?"

"I used to knit a lot, but I haven't held a pair of knitting needles in my hands in years. Why?"

"You'd be welcome to join our knitting circle. We meet on the second Friday of every month. Doesn't matter if you don't knit well. It's more of a social gathering than anything else, a chance for us women to talk without the men being around."

"That sounds perfect," Elizabeth said. "I'd love to."

"Wonderful. Do you have knitting needles and yarn?

"No. I didn't bring any with me."

Cammie came out from behind the counter and crossed to the far corner of the store. She plucked a pair of needles and a skein of brown yarn off a shelf and brought them back to Elizabeth. "Here," she said, shoving them into Elizabeth's hands. "Now you're ready."

"Oh…thank you…" Elizabeth set the needles and yarn onto the counter and moved to open her reticule.

Cammie's hand stopped her. "They're a gift. A welcome to Rocky Ridge gift."

Elizabeth was touched. She'd received many gifts in her life, but never one for no reason. She smiled at her new friend. "Thank you."

Cammie rushed back behind the counter and pulled out a piece of paper and a pencil, then wrote down the details. "You can either come to the store and go with me or I'll meet you there."

"I think I'd rather go with you, if you don't mind."

"Not at all."

After bidding Cammie goodbye, Elizabeth climbed into the wagon and drove off, her heart lighter than it had been on the way to town. She was thrilled that she'd made a new friend, and soon, she'd make many more. Her life in Rocky Ridge was falling into place just as she'd hoped it would.

And once Cole fell in love with her, her life would be perfect.

CHAPTER 8

*E*lizabeth jammed a clothespin on one of Cole's work shirts she was hanging on the clothes- line. Her hands were red and sore from all the scrubbing she'd done on the washboard that morning, but she didn't mind. She enjoyed taking care of Cole, cleaning the house and cooking for him.

She'd loved him for years, but with every new day as his wife, she fell more and more in love with him. She only wished she knew what to do so that he'd return it.

She'd been in Rocky Ridge for almost two weeks, and even though he was always kind and told her often how much he appreciated everything she did for him, he'd never made any advances toward her.

But she wouldn't give up, she told herself. Eventu- ally, he'd have to love her back. How could he not love someone who loved him as much as she did?

Quinn had gone to Denver for a few days, and Cole had invited Cy, Pete and TJ to eat with them. The aroma from the beef stew she'd prepared for the noon meal wafted through the open kitchen window. She'd baked fresh rolls, too, to soak up the gravy, so everything was ready for the men when they got back from moving some of the cattle to another pasture.

Bending forward, she pulled a blanket out of the basket of clean laundry to hang on the line. She was struggling to drape it across the rope when she heard Cole's voice behind her. "Do you need some help with that?"

She turned and smiled. Her heart jolted, as it always did when she saw him. She'd thought her reaction to him would ease with time, but so far, nothing had changed. "I wouldn't mind," she said. "I'm having trouble reaching."

He took the blanket from her hands and tossed half over the clothesline. As she watched, he straightened out the bunched-up sections and secured the blanket with clothespins.

"Anything else?" he asked, coming to stand in front of her.

She shook her head. "No, thank you. Lunch is ready whenever you are."

"The boys will be along in a minute."

Suddenly, a frown creased his forehead. He closed the gap between them and hooked his index finger under the cameo she was wearing around her neck. His finger against her bare skin sent a shiver of awareness through her and her breath hitched in her throat.

"Is that Sarah's necklace you're wearing?" he asked.

She looked down at his callused and work-roughened hand grazing her neck. "No," she said. "It's mine. We both have one."

"Oh." He removed his finger. "Since you planned to impersonate her, I wondered—"

She looked up at him, her throat dry. "You wondered if I'd stolen it from her."

"I'm sorry," he said, the tone of his voice contrite.

She was angry that he'd thought she was a thief, but at the same time, she could see why he'd thought it possible. After all, she had already admitted to stealing the letter he'd sent to Sarah. "We have so many of the same things. Too many," she said. "Whenever we got gifts, we got the same. I understand why. People don't want to appear to have favorites, and it's easier to buy two of something rather than to buy or make a gift that one of us might prefer over what the other got, especially since the gifts were given at the same time and we're both the same age. It does make sense, but when two people are expected to be exactly alike, it's hard to be an individual."

"I get the impression that's part of the reason you decided to take Sarah's place," he put in.

Elizabeth nodded. "I love Sarah. She's my sister, and she's also my best friend. But it was hard on both of us. Now, we won't be compared to each other and won't be expected to be the same person when we're so different."

"It must have been hard being treated the same when we all know you're no more alike than cake and turnip. You could handle a knife better than most of us and you didn't mind getting dirty. I couldn't imagine Sarah even thinking about either of those things."

"You always seemed to understand," she said quietly. "I never had to pretend to be something I'm not when I was with you."

That wasn't exactly true, but he didn't need to know she'd pretended every time they were together. She'd pretended that her feelings for him were nothing more than friendship, that he was nothing more to her than her sister's suitor, that she was happy for them both. And it looked like she'd have to go on pretending for the rest of her life.

"I'm glad you didn't," he said with a smile. "I liked that you were always so open and honest, not like some of the women I met at the parties and coming-out balls who only said what they thought they should, and what might help them land a rich husband."

She almost laughed. She'd been so dishonest, pretending she only wanted to be friends instead of pining for something she could never have. "I wasn't interested in landing any of them as a husband." That much was true. There was only one man who interested her, and he was smitten with her sister.

"I noticed that."

Voices interrupted their conversation. She looked away and saw Cy, Pete and TJ riding up. She set the bag of clothespins in the basket and picked it up. Turning away, she called back over her shoulder, "Now come and eat. By the time you wash up, I'll have the food on the table."

Elizabeth and Cole sat at the kitchen table after supper that night, a deck of cards between them.

He was teaching her how to play cribbage, a card game she'd heard of but never seen played.

"I learned to play it from a British soldier during the war," he told her. "We used small twigs poked into the mud to keep score. Nothing like a real board like this."

Elizabeth slid a glance at the intricately carved board on the table between them. Small holes were spaced along the surface of the board, a few of them holding wooden pegs. Her pegs were far behind Cole's.

"It's been around for a long time," he told her. "I think the rules have changed since it was first played, but—"

She giggled. "I have a feeling you've changed the rules to suit yourself."

Even though they'd spent the last two evenings playing the game after she'd finished washing the dishes and cleaning up, she'd still never won a game. She already owed him over a thousand dollars. Of course, the competition was all in fun.

They didn't spend much time alone together, and Elizabeth enjoyed their quiet time after supper, talking about what they'd done that day, what their plans were for the next day, their memories of their lives growing up back east.

As usual, he counted out his total points with the pegs on the board and sank his peg into the last hole, winning the game.

He grinned at her, his dark eyes boring into hers as she tallied how many points behind she was and added that number to the total she "owed" him.

"Since I don't think you have that kind of money to pay me," he said, "how are you ever going to make good on this debt?"

Her breath hitched. He was teasing. She knew that. So why did she get the impression he already had some idea of how he planned to collect?

Doing her best to keep her voice as light as his, she returned his smile and leaned forward across the table. "Perhaps I should stop playing until you tell me how I'll be expected to pay."

"I don't think that's necessary." He scooped up the cards and began to shuffle. "I'm sure we can come to some arrangement."

She couldn't keep her eyes off his work-roughened hands as they skillfully dealt the cards, wondering how they'd feel on her skin. Heat rose in her cheeks at her wayward thoughts and she looked away, focusing on the cards.

"Are you all right?" he asked, his brow furrowing. "Your face is suddenly flushed. Are you getting sick?"

She shook her head. "No. I'm fine, but I think I should retire before I owe you more than I already do."

"I like having you in debt to me," he said, wiggling his eyebrows and leaning forward. "I just need to find the perfect way for you to pay."

She leaned forward as well, their faces only inches apart. "Let me know when you decide."

For several long moments, there was no sound in the room other than their breaths mingling in the silence. Finally, he drew back and got up. "You're right. It's getting late," he said. "I'm going to check on the animals. I'll be back shortly."

"Then I'll see you in the morning. Goodnight."

As she readied herself for bed a few minutes later, she couldn't stop her thoughts from straying to the heat she'd seen in his eyes. He wanted her. She knew that now, and her heart soared. He cared about her. She just knew it.

Then her thoughts drifted to her debt, and how she could subtly suggest a way for her to pay him.

It had rained during the night, but the day of the barn raising dawned clear and warm. Elizabeth didn't know what to expect, only that there would be about thirty men working together and almost as many women to take care of feeding them.

"Are you sure I made enough food?" she asked as Cole set the last platter of roasted beef into the wagon.

"You aren't feeding everybody yourself," he replied with a chuckle. "There are other women bringing food, too."

She sighed. "I know, but I want to make a good impression."

"Then let's not be late." He took her hand to help her into the wagon. A rush of warmth spread through her at his touch, but she was getting used to it by now and didn't find herself blushing every time he touched her hand.

The construction was just getting started when they reached the Patterson ranch. She couldn't help but notice the mound of charred wood and ash that had once been their barn and the blackened earth around it. The fire that had consumed the barn had also threatened the house, so the new barn was being built closer to the creek running through the property.

Women were already bustling about, inside the house and out, carrying dishes and setting up tables in the shade of the oak trees dotting the yard.

"Can you manage to take the food into the house by yourself?" Cole asked once he'd helped her out of the wagon. "Or do you need me to come with you?"

Elizabeth slid a glance at the bed of the wagon,

filled with bowls and platters of food. She'd be more comfortable if he went inside with her and introduced her to the women, but she would never expect him to, since she knew he was anxious to join the men working on the foundation of the new barn.

"Of course I can manage," she lied. She'd fought her natural shyness her whole life, and facing these women alone made her heart race and her mouth go dry. She pasted a smile on her face and shooed him away.

She needn't have worried. She had just picked up a lemon pie out of the wagon when she heard a voice calling her name. She spun around, a smile lighting up her face when she saw Agnes Mulgrew shuffling across the yard.

"I was hoping you'd come," Agnes said, picking up a platter of beef and vegetables out of the wagon bed. "Come on, everyone's dying to meet Cole's pretty new bride."

As if she wasn't self-conscious enough, Elizabeth's stomach churned knowing she was going to be scrutinized by the other women.

"Don't worry, honey," Agnes said, patting her arm as they walked together toward the house. "They'll love you."

Elizabeth tried to smile, hoping her stomach would settle and she wouldn't embarrass herself.

Yet five minutes later, she wondered why she'd been so worried. The women greeted her as if she was a long-lost friend and her brain was spinning as she tried to remember all the names she'd heard and figure out the relationships to the men outside.

As if she'd known these women for years, she worked alongside them for the next three hours while they talked and laughed and enjoyed themselves.

Still, she missed spending time with Cole. How was she supposed to make him fall in love with her if they were always surrounded by other people?

She found herself wandering to the window to watch the work going on outside. Men's voices called out to each other over the sound of hammers and saws filling the air. Squinting into the sun, her gaze flitted from one man to the next, searching for the blue shirt she knew Cole was wearing.

Her stomach lurched when she finally caught sight of him, high on the rafters of the barn roof. If he fell… She couldn't bear to think of him being injured. Or worse. A cold chill washed over her and she spun around, unable to watch one second longer.

Isabella Morgan came up to stand beside her. "He's almost as handsome as Cade," she said with a grin.

She'd learned Cade and Isabella had been married for a few years, and even though Isabella still couldn't cook well, she had learned how to make an edible pound cake. Four cakes sat on the table waiting to be sliced.

"I hope you'll be as happy as we've been," Isabella went on. "It's not easy being a ranch wife, but with the right man, it's worth it."

"I'm sure you're right," Elizabeth agreed.

Bella looked past Elizabeth to the men working outside. "It's really coming along," she commented.

While Elizabeth hated to think of what could happen to Cole on the roof of the barn, at the same time, she couldn't stand not knowing what was happening. She turned and followed Bella's gaze. Her heart leapt into her throat and a gasp escaped her as she watched Cole begin to walk along a narrow beam, much like the tightrope walker she'd seen once when her aunt and uncle took her and Sarah to the circus in Philadelphia.

"Are you all right?" Bella asked. "You've gone very pale."

"Cole…it's very high…"

Bella nodded. "You're not alone. Most of us feel the same way when our men are up there."

Elizabeth couldn't prevent the loud sigh of relief that escaped her when he made it safely to the other end of the beam, then began to climb down the ladder to the ground.

He took off his shirt, and his tanned skin gleamed in the sunshine. Although she was a fair distance away, she was mesmerized by him and imagined his strong muscles moving beneath his skin.

"Looks like the men are stopping for lunch," Minnie Patterson called out. "Let's get them fed so they can get back to work."

The rest of the day sped by in a whirlwind of activity until finally the barn was finished, the dishes had been washed, dried and returned to their rightful owners, and Cole and Elizabeth were on their way home.

"Did you enjoy yourself today?" Cole asked as he guided the wagon toward their ranch. He was pleased with how Bee had fit in with the other ranchers' wives. Not that he'd expected anything less. She'd always been one of the most popular girls he'd known back in Summerton.

She shifted in the wagon seat to face him. "I did. It was a lot of work for us women, but no more than what you men accomplished. And work is always easier with company."

"That's true." He had to admit he'd been a bit worried, though, that she might let something slip about the circumstances of their marriage.

He should have trusted Bee more. She'd likely be just as careful as he was and wouldn't want to be the subject of the gossip that would result if the truth got out.

But he couldn't imagine living this lie his entire life. And he doubted Bee would want that, either. He made a mental note to talk to her about it once they got home.

Dusk was falling, and clouds had rolled in late that afternoon. Hopefully, they'd make it home before it started to rain.

"Are you tired?" he asked.

"No more tired than you are, I'm sure," she said.

"I've never seen anything like what went on today. That a whole building could be built in one day."

"Well, it's not a live-in kind of building, just a shell really."

"Still, it was amazing to watch. I've only been here a short time, but already I can't imagine ever going back east to live. The air, the land, the people here…I feel as if I can be my true self here. The ladies I met today aren't interested in parties, and shopping, and making the best financial match when it comes to marrying. I'm going to love living here. I just know it."

"I'm glad." And he was. They would have other problems to deal with, but at least that wouldn't be one of them. A few of his friends had married women from back east, and within months, they'd left and gone back.

At least Bee seemed happy. And, he had to admit, that made him happy. He couldn't say exactly when or how that had happened, but somehow her happiness had become important to him.

A raindrop hit his nose, drawing him out of his thoughts. "Looks like we might not make it."

She grinned. "Worried about getting wet?"

"Not me," he replied. "I was concerned about you."

"Me? A little rain never hurt anybody," she said with a laugh. "Don't you remember the day we got caught in the rain at the county fair? And we ran through the puddles—"

Suddenly, she stopped speaking and turned away.

"When was that?" he asked. "I don't remember ever

running through puddles with you. Sarah and I got caught in the rain a few times, and once, when we were about fourteen, she convinced me to splash in the puddles with her. I was surprised that she'd do that, because she was always so prim and proper, but we laughed until we cried. But I don't remember ever doing that with you."

"Oh…of course…I was thinking about Reginald and I," she sputtered. "Silly me. It is fun, though, isn't it?"

He nodded, smiling. That day had been one of the best days of his life.

A few more drops fell, and before long, the skies opened and the rain teemed down.

By the time they reached the ranch house, they were both soaked. As he helped Bee out of the wagon, he couldn't help noticing how her wet clothes clung to her, outlining every curve.

She was still smiling, lifting her face up to the sky and letting the warm rain pour over her. Without a thought, she pulled the pins from her hair and shook her head. Her hair tumbled down her back.

Fire surged through him, settling low in his belly. He wanted her. Her. Not Sarah, but Bee. Wanted to hold her, to touch her, to make love to her.

"What is it?" she asked, noticing the way he was staring at her. "Why are you looking at me like that?"

He shook his head. She'd never believe him if he told her how pretty she looked at that moment, soaked to the skin. "Nothing," he said, his voice cracking. "You'd better get inside before you catch a cold."

"There are puddles all over the yard," she said.

"You aren't thinking what I think you're thinking—"

"I am," she said, grabbing his hand and drawing him toward a large puddle beside the house. "I dare you."

His brows lifted. "You dare me?"

"Are you too old to play?"

He considered it for a minute. His days were filled with hard work and most nights, when he and Bee weren't playing cards, he spent his time doing paperwork or reading.

Old? She thought he was old? He couldn't resist the challenge in her eyes. "Not at all," he said a moment before he jumped into the puddle, sending up a spray of muddy water. It splattered Bee, and instead of being upset, she laughed. Loudly. A moment or two later, she joined him in the puddle, and within seconds, they were both covered in mud.

Bee's squeals and their laughter filled the air as they ran through the yard, splashing into every puddle they could find until they were both exhausted.

Finally, they slowed and stopped at the bottom of the stairs. Even though it was growing dark and he could barely see her features, he knew her face would be flushed and her eyes would be sparkling with merriment.

She was covered in mud. A clump of mud clung to

her chin. He reached up and wiped it off. His fingers grazed her skin, and he heard her breath catch.

She gazed up at him, an invitation in her eyes.

He didn't want to kiss her, didn't want to think about how soft her lips had felt beneath his after the wedding, didn't want to feel himself responding to her. He loved Sarah. Only Sarah.

But if that was true, why did he find himself looking forward to getting home at night to see Bee? Why did he itch to wrap her hair around his fingers? To feel her skin beneath his touch?

"Is something wrong?" he heard her ask as if she was a mile away instead of right in front of him, a tiny frown marring her brow.

"Nothing's wrong. Nothing at all," he murmured as he gave in to the temptation and lowered his lips to hers.

CHAPTER 9

He was going to kiss her. Elizabeth couldn't believe it was really going to happen. Her first real kiss. Well, the kiss at the stage-coach depot had been real enough, but she'd been so shocked she didn't even have time for what was happening to register in her brain. Besides, the kiss hadn't been intended for her. Still, it had practically curled her toes and singed her eyelashes right off.

Then there was the kiss after the wedding, if the slight brush of his lips could be called a kiss. In her mind, even though he'd known who she was, that wasn't a real kiss, not the kind of kiss she'd heard about from her friends who'd already married.

This time, though, Cole had no reason to kiss her, no wedding ceremony where a kiss was expected, nothing but the fact that he wanted to. And he wanted to kiss *her,* not Sarah.

Her breath caught in her throat as he cupped her chin and raised her lips to meet his. He smelled of rain, and tasted of the coffee he'd had before they'd left the Pattersons'.

She couldn't breathe. Her body tingled from the top of her head to the tips of her toes. Fire swept through her veins, making her legs tremble and her body turn to liquid.

She'd never experienced anything like it. This was the kind of kiss she'd dreamed of, but more. So much more.

His arms wrapped around her and she clung to him as he deepened the kiss. His tongue traced the seam of her lips. She wasn't sure exactly what he wanted from her, so she parted them slightly. His tongue invaded her mouth, seeking, plundering her own. The sensation was exquisite. A sound escaped from her throat. Or was it from his? She couldn't tell. She heard his sharp intake of breath a moment before he suddenly released her and took a step back. "You'd better go inside."

Elizabeth's breathing was ragged, the sudden loss of his warmth sending a shiver through her. For a few seconds, she could only stare at him, at his lips. "What?" she asked finally.

"Go inside, Bee."

Had her kissing skills been so terrible he couldn't stand to even look at her now? She didn't have any experience, but she was more than willing to learn. It seemed he wasn't interested, though. Her heart sank like a lead weight into her stomach. "Aren't you coming?"

"I'll be in later."

"Why—?"

"Please, Bee. Just do as I ask."

Tears pricked her eyes. Over the past few days, she'd come to believe that maybe, just maybe, he was starting to care for her. When he'd kissed her, the thought had flitted through her mind that this was the beginning of a new chapter in their relationship. That their marriage might become real after all. But she'd been wrong. So wrong.

Desperately trying to hide the pain of rejection tearing her apart inside, she spun around and raced up the porch stairs. She heard a curse spill from his lips as she hurried into the house and slammed the door behind her.

"What was I thinking, Dusty?" Cole asked the honey-colored mare standing in front of him a few minutes later. "I wasn't thinking, and that's the problem. I don't think when I'm around her."

Cole picked up a brush and began to run it down Dusty's coat. Dusty turned his head to look at Cole, then nickered as if he understood Cole's dilemma perfectly.

Cole should never have kissed Bee. Should never have let himself get drawn into her playfulness. Really, sloshing through puddles like a little boy. Only once before had he been persuaded to act like that, and that had been with Sarah. They'd laughed and giggled like little children, but when they were soaked and he'd walked her home, he remembered she'd been overly quiet.

He'd laughed with Bee, too, but instead of letting it go at that, he'd kissed her.

Her lips had tasted of cherries and cocoa from the pie she'd eaten at the Pattersons'. And her body, her clothes like a second skin, had made him lose all common sense.

How could he have been unfaithful to Sarah? Until Bee showed up, the thought of letting himself love someone else had never occurred to him in all the time he and Sarah had been apart. True, he hadn't seen her in six years, and since he'd changed and Bee had changed, it was likely Sarah had, too.

Sarah sure wouldn't have fit in as well in Rocky Ridge as Bee had, and he couldn't imagine her pitching in with the barn raising like Bee had. Sarah would have been a perfect hostess, though, as long as someone else did the work. Bee had never once complained, no matter what.

But Bee was keeping something from him. Every once in a while, it seemed as if she was about to say something, then stopped herself. He couldn't imagine what kind of thing she'd be worried about telling him, since that was one of the best parts of their friendship—

they could tell each other anything and not be judged. He hoped he'd just imagined it. He'd hate to think that had changed, too.

Setting the brush on a shelf, he crossed the barn and scooped out a bucketful of oats. "And who the hell is Reginald?" he muttered as he set the bucket down in Dusty's stall. "I grew up with Bee and Sarah. I knew their friends, and I never once heard of anybody called Reginald."

His stomach twisted with jealousy. "Well, Dusty," he said, leading the horse into his stall and closing the gate. "I think Bee and I need to have a little talk."

Elizabeth busied herself putting the leftover food away, doing her best to keep her mind off the kiss she'd just shared with Cole.

He'd kissed her. Not Sarah. Things had changed between them over the past few days, but there was still no question in her mind that his heart belonged to her twin. So why had he kissed her? The touch of his lips had aroused sensations inside her that she hadn't known even existed.

She heard the door open a few moments before Cole appeared in the kitchen doorway, leaving wet footprints on her clean floor. "Cole!" she cried out. "Your boots!"

He looked down, then raised his head to look at her. "I don't really care about the floor right now, and I'll clean it up when we're done. Right now, I want to know who Reginald is."

Elizabeth's heart flipped in her chest. Reginald had been the first name that popped into her mind when she almost slipped and admitted it had been her and Cole who'd raced through the puddles at the fair so many years ago.

"Why?"

He didn't answer her question, but added another. "Reginald who?"

Oh, heavens, she thought, he was going to force her to add one lie on top of another. *Think fast, Elizabeth.* "Well,…" she began, "I met him at the fair. Don't you remember?" Perhaps she could convince him he had a bad memory.

"No, I don't. When did you meet him? How?"

Elizabeth waved away his questions. "It was so long ago I don't even remember the details." If she wasn't careful, she'd trip herself up. The only solution was to distract him. "Now, how would you like a piece of pie and a cup of coffee?"

"If you remember splashing through puddles with him, surely you remember a few details. Like his last name. How you met him. How well you knew him when you went off with him to splash through those puddles."

Why was he being so insistent on knowing the details of that night? And why did he care who Reginald was?

"Really, Cole, what I did or didn't do before our marriage isn't important. I didn't do anything to damage my reputation, if that's what you're concerned about."

A slight tinge of color washed over his face. "Uh… no…I didn't mean to imply…"

"Then if you're finished with your interrogation, I'm going to bed."

"Wait a minute—"

"Goodnight, Cole." Hurrying away before he had a chance to ask any more questions she didn't have answers for, she left him standing in the kitchen and raced up the stairs to her bedroom.

She closed the door behind her and leaned against it until her heart rate returned to normal and her breathing slowed.

She wasn't good at lying, and she was sure if she'd stayed longer, she would have slipped and the truth would have come out. She couldn't risk that. Not yet.

By Tuesday morning, Elizabeth's nerves were ready to snap. As she whipped up a bowl of eggs and kept an eye on the bacon sizzling in the skillet on the stove, her thoughts drifted back to Cole's kiss. Ever since, something had changed between them—an awareness that had affected the easy friendship they'd shared since the day they'd met just after she and Sarah had moved to Summerton after their parents' deaths.

Every time she looked at Cole, she remembered his arms around her, his lips on hers, the tingles that shot through her body at his touch. He'd felt something, too. She was sure of it. Several times over the past few days, she'd caught him watching her, studying her as if he'd never seen her before.

But the kiss had never been mentioned, almost as if it had never happened.

She hummed a melody of an old song she remembered from her childhood as she set the bowl down on the worktable and reached for two plates on the shelf. She turned, and when she saw him standing in the doorway, couldn't prevent a squeak of surprise. "Oh, my goodness, you frightened me standing there."

"I didn't mean to," he said, pulling out a chair and sitting down. "Was that *Annie Laurie?*" he asked.

She nodded and smiled softly. "Do you like it?"

"That's Sarah's favorite song."

Elizabeth shook her head, then turned to check the bacon in the skillet. With a fork, she moved it around to cook it evenly. "No, she hated that song. Said it depressed her."

"She sang it for me a few times—"

Heat surged into Elizabeth's cheeks. What could she say?

"What's going on, Bee?" Cole asked. "You're hiding something, and I want to know what it is.

"No—"

He got up and closed the gap between them, took the

skillet out of her hand and set it aside. Then he gripped her shoulders, gently but firmly. "I won't have secrets between us. Tell me."

Was this the right time? She wasn't sure, but she hated the way things were between them now, and maybe her confession might be for the best. She nodded. "All right, but you have to remember we were little more than children. We didn't know any better at first."

He didn't speak, but he did release her and sat down at the table. Elizabeth crossed and sat opposite him, crossing her hands on the table. For a moment, she stared down, trying to decide where to start.

"When Sarah and I were young, we discovered most people couldn't tell us apart." She let out a brittle laugh. "Some people never did see the differences even as adults."

"I was one of those people who couldn't tell one of you from the other. The only way I knew who was who was because you were both so opposite on the inside."

"Exactly," Elizabeth said. "We got so tired of people confusing us, and having to tell people which twin we were. The first time we switched places was when Sarah was invited to go on a hayride and a barn dance at a farm outside town. She didn't want to go, but she'd agreed to. I told her I'd go in her place."

"Did you go?"

She nodded. "I had a lovely time. Of course, I had to pretend I was Sarah, but that wasn't too difficult. No one knew the difference. After that, we switched places often, especially when one of us wanted to do something—or didn't want to. We managed to trick our tutors, our friends, even Aunt Meg."

For a few seconds, Cole stared at her. She could almost see the truth dawning on him. Finally, he leaned back in his chair and folded his arms across his chest. "And me? You two played your tricks on me, too?"

She nodded. "I'm sorry, Cole. There were times Sarah had made arrangements to see you, but changed her mind. I took her place."

Silence fell in the room. Only the birds chirping outside and the occasional crowing of a rooster broke it.

"So the song you were humming, the dance we had that I couldn't remember, the kisses—"

"No! Not the kisses. I never let you kiss me, well, until the day I got off the stage. I wouldn't have gone that far." Not that she hadn't wanted to, more than anything. But she would never betray her sister's trust.

"The puddles…"

She gave him a wan smile. "That was me."

"So there is no Reginald."

"No."

"I see."

"I know it was wrong of us…but I was never able to refuse Sarah…and she didn't want to hurt you…"

He laughed then, a short, sarcastic laugh as he got up, his chair scraping across the floor. "Right."

"I seem to constantly be apologizing to you," she said. "I really am sorry."

"I hope you both enjoyed yourselves."

There was nothing she could say. They'd been wrong, and their only defense was that they were young and foolish. Still, by the thunderous expression on Cole's face, it was obvious he wasn't going to forgive her any time soon.

Only a few clouds dotted the sky when Elizabeth woke on Friday morning. She bustled around the kitchen, setting the table while slices of bread soaked to make French toast.

Since her confession to Cole about the tricks she and Sarah had played on him, he'd been cold and distant. Whether he was hurt or just angry, she didn't know, but either way, she was the cause, and she didn't know what to do about it.

She'd apologized. She'd gone out of her way to cook his favorite meals and had tried to be cheerful and easy-going. What more could she do?

Their after-dinner card games had stopped. Cole spent more time than usual outside after supper, and when he did finally come inside, he disappeared into the small room he used as an office and stayed there until she went to bed.

Elizabeth had even waited the night before hoping they would have time to talk after he finished the paper-work he'd told her he had to take care of. While she'd waited, she'd practiced her knitting. She was slow, but at least she hadn't dropped any stitches.

She'd finally given up and gone to bed, but she was still awake when she heard his footsteps on the stairs. She'd thought about getting up and confronting him, but decided against it. For years, he'd been duped, and he needed time to forgive her.

She'd been looking forward to going to town and joining Cammie at the knitting circle, but now, knowing she was leaving Cole angry with her, some of the enjoyment had faded.

"If you'd rather I didn't go into town today—" she began as she set a plate of bacon and eggs in front of him.

"That's no problem," he replied.

"I'll be sure to be back early. I've left cold fried chicken and biscuits for your noon meal, and if you don't mind, we'll have leftover stew for supper. I'll make dumplings to go in it."

"That's fine. Don't rush." He stabbed a slice of bacon with his fork.

She crossed to the table and wrapped her hand around his, holding it in mid-air. "We need to talk about this. I don't want you to be angry with me."

He gazed up at her, his dark eyes searching her face. "I don't want to be angry," he said quietly, "but—"

"I know what we did was wrong."

"It was."

"At the time, we didn't think it would hurt anyone."

"And now?"

She sighed and released his hand. "Now I see the damage I did by pretending to be Sarah, but my intentions were good. You were my friend. I didn't want to see you hurt."

Cole set his fork down on the plate. "I understand that and I appreciate it, but it would have been better to find out the truth earlier rather than later. I wouldn't have spent years believing she loved me."

"I know. And I'm so sorry for my part in that. I don't know what to do so you'll forgive me. We were always friends." Tears pricked her eyes and she brushed them away with the back of her hand. "I don't want to lose that."

And any chance of being something more, she wanted to add, but stopped herself. This wasn't the time.

CHAPTER 10

After a few minutes of being introduced to the other ladies in the large kitchen of Virginia Morgan's boarding house, Elizabeth felt as if she'd known them her whole life, even if she was having trouble remembering all the names and the family relationships some of them shared.

Cammie squeezed her hand as she introduced yet another woman who had just entered the room to join the group. "Don't worry," she said with a chuckle. "Soon you'll know everyone in town.

"That's true," Olivia Mitchell put in, tucking a stray strand of pale blonde hair behind her ear. "I've only lived in Rocky Ridge a short time, but everyone is so friendly and welcoming that I feel as if I've lived here forever."

"Olivia just got married," Cammie interjected. "To Landry Mitchell, the blacksmith."

Cammie picked up a skein of yarn off a chair beside her and patted the seat for Olivia to sit down. "One day, you'll have to tell her the story about how you and Landry got together, Olivia."

Olivia's cheeks pinked, but she grinned at her friend. "I'm sure Bee will hear all about it soon enough."

Conversation drifted to the latest happenings in town as more ladies joined them. Names blurred together— Petunia Morse, Katie McLennan, Virginia Morgan...

A woman Elizabeth suspected was about her aunt's age filled one of the two only empty chairs left and heaved a breath. "Heavens, I swear those steps are getting harder and harder to climb every day," she said, her eyes twinkling. "I'm sure it has nothing to do with me getting older. And absolutely has nothing to do with the cookies and cakes I've been baking for Buck."

Then, apparently noticing Elizabeth for the first time, she bounded out of her chair and rounded the table. "I'm Maude Lang," she said, taking Elizabeth's hand in hers. "Maude to my friends. You're Cole Berringer's new bride, aren't you?"

Elizabeth nodded.

"I thought so," Maude went on. "I didn't get a chance to meet you at the wedding. You're a lucky woman. Why, if I was thirty years younger..."

Laughter erupted at the table. "You wouldn't have paid any attention to Cole then either," one of the ladies —Petunia, Elizabeth thought that was her name—interrupted, then leaned closer to Elizabeth. "Maude has been waiting for Buck Morgan to pop the question since she got to town, but the man is slower than molasses."

"A snail moves faster," Maude said with a sigh, "but he'll get there. Even snails have to reach their destination, eventually. And when he does…"

"We'll be knitting baby booties?" one of the women piped up.

"Oh, heavens, no. I'll leave the child-raising to you youngsters."

The door opened then and the last member of the group bustled in, a large bag on her arm and carrying a tray covered with a cloth. She set the tray in the center of the table and plopped down into the last chair. "It's been such a busy morning I barely had time to get these into the oven."

Cammie introduced Elizabeth to the newcomer, Nell Davidson. She and her husband ran the telegraph office.

"I'm so glad Cammie happened to mention you were coming today," Nell said to Elizabeth, digging into her bag and pulling out a battered envelope. "I have a letter for Cole so I'll just give it to you and save myself a ride out to the ranch."

"Of course," she replied with a smile. "I'd be happy to take it for you."

Elizabeth's smile faded and she felt the blood drain from her face when Nell slid the envelope across the table. The letter was addressed to Cole—in Sarah's oh-so-perfect penmanship.

"Are you all right, dear?" Maude took her hand.

"Why, you look like you've just had a terrible shock. Your hands are like ice. Quick, Virginia, get Bee a cup of hot sweet tea."

"No…really…I'm fine…" She was anything but fine. Her stomach churned at the thought of what was written on the letter inside the envelope. How had Sarah known where to find her? Why was she writing to Cole? Had she changed her mind and decided to accept his proposal?

It was too late, of course. Cole was married to her.

"I hope it's nothing serious, but if it is, please let me know if there's anything I can do."

Elizabeth nodded. "Thank you, but I'm sure it's just news from home."

Plastering a smile on her face, she tucked the letter into the pocket of her skirt. "Now, I'd much rather knit and get to know you all better."

"Don't you think it's exciting to get letters from far away?" Cammie let out a dreamy sigh. "I can't wait to go and live somewhere else like you did."

"You're better off here," Nell said. "The things I hear about other places—"

"I think it's wonderful to have a home where you have family and good friends," Virginia added. "I'm so thankful I married Will. I have a huge family now, instead of just me and Jeremy."

As the afternoon wore on, Elizabeth found herself relaxing and enjoying the companionship of the circle.

Maude shared her hand-written pattern for a winter hat and helped her cast on enough stitches.

"I'll make this for Cole," she announced, "for Christmas."

"Christmas?" three women said at once.

"That's months away," Virginia added.

Elizabeth laughed. "It'll likely take me that long to finish."

The hours sped by with tea, cookies, conversation and laughter. All too soon, the ladies began to pack up their belongings, their monthly get-together over until the next time.

A few minutes later, Elizabeth was driving out of town toward the ranch, dreading the moment when she'd have to give Cole the letter from the woman he really loved.

Cole paused in his digging, leaning on the handle of the shovel. For the past ten minutes, he'd been telling Quinn about the tricks Sarah and Elizabeth had played on them both over the years. "They fooled us time and time again," he said, straightening and ramming the shovel into the hardened earth.

Quinn laughed, garnering a frown from Cole. "You're not mad?"

Quinn shook his head. "What's the point of being

mad at something that happened years ago? And really, you have to admit it was pretty ingenious. I bet we would have done the same thing if we looked enough alike to get away with it."

Cole had to admit he was probably right. There were plenty of times when he was growing up that he would have been happy to let someone else pretend to be him.

"They were young, and I'm sure it seemed like fun," Quinn went on.

"That's true, I suppose," Cole admitted. "But it does make me question everything now."

Quinn scooped up a shovelful of dirt and tossed it into the pile beside the hole they were digging. "What do you mean?"

"From what Bee told me, some of my memories of Sarah were actually memories of Bee."

Quinn dug the shovel into the dirt and looked over at Cole, his brows lifting. "Like what?"

"Like dancing with Bee at her sixteenth birthday party when I thought I was dancing with Sarah. Like running through the rain and jumping in puddles while we got soaked. Like—"

Quinn held his hand up to stop Cole's reminiscences. "Okay. I see what you mean."

"The trouble is, I was wrong about a lot of the reasons I think I fell in love with Sarah. Times I was so happy just to be with her, to talk to her, were times it wasn't Sarah at all. It was Bee."

Quinn let out a slow whistle. "That makes it awkward, doesn't it?"

"Now I don't know who I really loved," Cole said. "There were times Sarah's attitude really irritated me, but was I with Sarah or Bee? Which twin was I with? I can't remember every single minute we were together so I can ask Bee about them."

"That's true," Quinn agreed. "All you can do now is to look at Bee and know she's the one you're with. There are no more tricks, no more substitutions."

"She told me about a few times we were together that I thought I was with Sarah. What bothers me most is that those times were some of the best times *Sarah* and I had together."

"But they were really Bee, not Sarah?" Quinn asked.

Cole nodded. "That's what I said."

Quinn shook his head in disbelief. "I see your problem now. Hard to say which twin you really fell for, isn't it?"

"Loving Bee would be a disaster," Cole protested, even though he couldn't help thinking about how his life had changed for the better since she'd arrived in Rocky Ridge. She worked from dawn until dusk—and sometimes later. She never complained. She was willing to do whatever needed to be done to make the ranch a success, and to make his life easier.

And he enjoyed his evenings with her. They talked, they laughed, they teased each other, just like the old days. Being with her was…comfortable. Well, except for the fact that he wanted her in his bed.

That had come as a surprise to him, but he couldn't deny it. He'd thought it was because she reminded him so much of Sarah, but the reality of it was that it was her he wanted, not Sarah.

Yes, he'd admit his marriage to Bee had made his life so much better. But… Where were the buts?

Quinn let out a chuckle, then picked up the shovel and resumed his digging. "If you made a mistake, even one you didn't know you were making at the time, be thankful you know now. Bee is here, and maybe if you let yourself, you'd realize you've loved her all along."

Cole turned away and jammed the shovel into the dirt. Impossible! Or was it? Had he been wrong all along?

As he worked on the fence line for the rest of the afternoon, Quinn's words echoed in his brain. And by the time the sun dipped low on the mountain peaks in the distance, he had to admit to himself that it was quite possible Quinn was absolutely right.

By the time Cole got back to the house for supper that night, his mood had brightened considerably. He still hadn't figured out exactly what was happening between him and Bee, but he was tired of trying to make sense of it.

The tricks Bee and Sarah had pulled on him were childish, but as Quinn had reminded him more than once that afternoon, the girls were young at the time. They hadn't meant any harm. They'd thought it was fun.

Cole had never been one to hold a grudge, but he had been harboring ill will toward Bee the past few days. It was time to let it go. Her words from the other morning came back to him. She didn't want to lose their friendship. And when he really thought about it, he didn't want to lose the closeness they'd both shared either.

Bee's friendship had been one of the few good things in his life growing up. His father was a drunkard, his mother a worn woman who did her best to stay out of the way when his father came home from the mill at night. Cole and Quinn had learned very early on that when his father was home, they were better off anywhere else.

Especially at the Mains' house, where there was love and peace, not to mention more food than he could stuff himself with.

Putting the memories back where they belonged, Cole opened the door and went inside, breathing in the sweet aroma of apples and cinnamon meeting his nose. He hung his hat on the hook behind the door and followed the mouth-watering smell to the kitchen.

For a few seconds, he leaned against the doorway and watched Bee bustle around the kitchen. Flour smudged her cheek, and her face glowed with a faint sheen of perspiration from standing over the stove.

A strange longing filled him as he looked at her. He

wanted her in his bed. He was well aware of how the sight of her conjured up impure thoughts every single time. But it was more than that. He wanted…what? He couldn't define it, only knew that there was something missing inside him, an ache that he was discovering more every day that only she could ease.

Elizabeth turned, her eyes widening and her heartbeat skipping a beat when she caught sight of him standing in the doorway, watching her. Her cheeks pinked as his gaze swept over her. "Supper's ready whenever you are," she said.

"Smells good." He straightened to allow her through the opening with the bowl of stew. Her hip brushed against him, and fire raced through his belly, settling low.

"Sit down and eat before it gets cold," she said over her shoulder. "I'll get the bread."

Cole followed her to the dining room and sat down, his gaze landing on the envelope. "What's this?"

"A letter from Sarah." Oh, how she wished she could have hidden it and pretended she'd never seen it. She couldn't, though. Surely Nell would have mentioned it to him next time he ran into her in town.

His face darkened, and his brow furrowed. "What does she want?"

"I don't know. I didn't open it," Elizabeth said. "It's addressed to you."

He slid it away from his plate and picked up his fork as Elizabeth ladled out the stew and dumplings onto his plate. Without giving it another glance, he picked up a thick slice of bread, and slathered it with butter. He took a bite and let out a moan of satisfaction as he chewed. "I swear, Bee, you make the best bread I've ever had."

"I'm glad you like it," she replied. "Now please open the letter."

"After supper."

Elizabeth sighed. She wouldn't ruin the evening by pestering him to open it. She'd just have to wait until he was ready.

"Tell me about your day," he said between bites of stew. "Did you enjoy your afternoon in town with the ladies?"

The tone of his voice was friendlier than she'd heard it since the night he'd kissed her, and her heart lightened. She had no idea what had brought on the change, but she wasn't going to question it. Had he decided to forgive her? If he had, perhaps their relationship could get back to where it was before. She hoped so. "It was wonderful," she replied, picking up the bowl of dumplings and the bread and carrying it past him to the table. "I met so many women, and they're all so nice…"

For the rest of the meal, they fell into a familiar and comfortable conversation, just like they used to have when they lived in Summerton. Still, her eyes kept drifting to the letter on the table, as if she expected it to explode at any moment.

Finally, Cole drained his coffee and leaned back in the chair. "I know you've had a busy day, and I appreciate that you still found time to make a good meal."

"I'm happy to do it," she replied. And she was. She'd never thought she'd find such joy in looking after Cole—or any man, for that matter—but since she'd come to Rocky Ridge, she'd found she was happy keeping house for Cole and taking part in simple activities like the knitting circle.

Only one thing was missing—Cole's love.

The letter again drew her attention. Cole noticed her staring at the envelope and picked it up. His expression darkened. "I should just throw it into the fire," he said, his voice gruff and low.

She couldn't help being pleased he felt that way, but still, something stopped her from letting him burn it. "No!"

"Why not?" His eyes bored into hers. "I'm not interested in anything she has to say."

"It could be important."

"All right, I'll open it, but only because you asked me to," he said as he slipped his finger under the flap and tore it open. He took out a single sheet of paper, his brow furrowing as his eyes skimmed over the contents.

Then he handed the letter to Elizabeth. Her gaze scanned the words on the page. A sense of dread washed over her, and she looked up at Cole. "They're coming here…Aunt Meg and Sarah…they're coming here. But why?"

"Guess we'll find out when they get here." Cole got up and rounded the table to stand over her He drew her to her feet and cupped her chin in his hand, forcing her to meet his eyes. "It'll be fine," he said softly, then brushed his lips over hers. "I promise."

She gazed up at him, lost in his dark depths. She nodded slightly, praying he meant it.

CHAPTER 11

"I've been thinking," Cole said early one morning a few days later while they were eating breakfast.

Elizabeth's brows lifted but she grinned. "Oh? What about?"

"Us."

Her heart tripped. He hadn't seemed overly upset at the prospect of Sarah's visit, but she hadn't spent much time alone with him since the letter arrived. Cole had been kept busy from dawn until dusk moving the cattle to new pastures to graze, while she'd been furiously cleaning and cooking in preparation for Aunt Meg and Sarah's arrival. She'd even stayed up late at night sewing new curtains for the kitchen window and a matching tablecloth.

"What about us?" She recognized the threadiness

creeping into her voice. She moved her fork around her plate, her appetite gone.

"Sarah and your aunt will be here tomorrow," he began. "Have you given any thought to the sleeping arrangements?"

"We have enough bedrooms—"

"I meant *our* sleeping arrangements."

Heat rose in Elizabeth's cheeks. "Why...I..."

"How much of our situation are you planning to share with them?" he asked.

"I hadn't given it much thought. Of course they're going to know we got married."

"Will you also tell them we don't have a real marriage?"

"Oh..." *Heavens!* They shouldn't even be discussing the intimate side of their marriage. It was... not exactly improper, but definitely an uncomfortable subject.

She bounded up and hurried into the kitchen on the pretense of getting the coffeepot off the stove. "More coffee?" she asked.

"Sure," he replied, sliding his cup closer to her as she brought the coffeepot back into the dining room.

"Cream? Sugar?"

"Bee!"

The sharp tone of his voice stopped her in her tracks.

"You know I don't take cream and sugar," he said. "Are you embarrassed to talk about this?"

"Well..."

"We've been friends forever, and now we're husband and wife. I want us to be able to talk about anything and everything."

She nodded. "You're right." She sat back down and looked down at her hands. Weeks of scrubbing clothes with harsh soap, washing dishes, and all the other chores she did on a daily basis had made them rough and callused. Yet she didn't care. She'd gladly done everything she had for the man she loved, even if he didn't love her back.

"You've been so caught up in a cooking and cleaning whirlwind, that's why I did the thinking for us," he teased. "You'll have to decide today how much you're going to tell them."

She gazed up at him. "I'd like them to think we're happily married."

"Then don't you think they'll wonder why we aren't sharing a bedroom?"

"I suppose they will."

"So, why don't you move your things into my room while they're here?"

"And share a bed?"

"We've done it before." A twinkle appeared in his eyes, but he didn't comment on the circumstances surrounding their one night in bed together.

He drained his coffee cup and got up. "I'll come in for supper early tonight in case you need any help with anything."

Rounding the table, he leaned down and brushed his

lips against hers. Lately, he'd made a point of giving her a quick kiss before he left. She had no idea what had prompted this new habit, and as she packed up her clothing and toiletries later that day and moved them to Cole's room, she made a decision. Assuming Sarah and Aunt Meg went back to Summerton, and assuming she was still Cole's wife by the time they left, she wouldn't be going back to her own bedroom. She was in Cole's bed to stay.

Elizabeth's stomach was in a knot the size of a hangman's noose as she stood on the boardwalk watching the stagecoach roll to a stop in front of the Wells Fargo office. Cole's face was set in stone, his hands deep in his pockets. They'd barely spoken all the way into town, each of them lost in their own thoughts.

While Elizabeth was thrilled to see her sister and her aunt again, she was terrified of what changes in her life the visit might bring. Was this the beginning of the end of her marriage? How would people react to learning the truth about her and Sarah? Were Sarah and Aunt Meg angry with her?

No, they couldn't be angry, she decided. If they were, why would they spend so much time traveling west to see her?

Elizabeth had spent the past week scrubbing and scouring every inch of the ranch house to prepare for their visit. It wasn't as big or as grand as Aunt Meg's house in Summerton. There were no servants to do their bidding, and the mercantile didn't offer the selection in food and other dry goods they'd find back east. Still, she was proud of what she'd accomplished in the house since her arrival and was thrilled to have made new friends.

Now that she thought about it, she hadn't seen any sign of Delia and Cornelia Moore since they'd parted ways the day she arrived. Strange, she thought, since Rocky Ridge was such a small town. She made a mental note to make an effort to see them once Aunt Meg and Sarah went home.

As she watched, Sarah's head popped out of the stagecoach window and her arm waved furiously.

"Bee!" Sarah's voice carried over the now-familiar sounds of horses and wagons in the street.

A wide grin tugged at Elizabeth's lips. Oh, how she'd missed her sister. She was happy in Rocky Ridge, but she felt as if her other half was missing.

She only hoped Cole had meant it when he'd told her again that morning that everything would be fine.

Cole busied himself gathering up the trunks and loading them into the wagon while Bee, Sarah and her aunt greeted each other, hugging and all talking at once.

All his plans and goals for years had been made

with Sarah in mind, and ever since he'd gotten the letter, he'd both dreaded and looked forward to seeing her again.

Would all those old feelings surge up again? Would he regret marrying Bee? Wish he'd waited for Sarah?

Now, she was finally here. So why wasn't his heart thundering in his chest the way it used to? Why weren't his insides turning inside out with desire?

The truth came to him like a kick from an ornery mule. He was married to Bee, and even though he'd fought it, he was happy. He'd fallen in love with his substitute bride.

A smile quirked his lips when he looked at the two of them together. So alike in looks, yet so different. Sarah was dressed in a dark red elegant traveling suit and had a feathery hat perched on her pale yellow curls. Bee, on the other hand, wore a simple emerald green cotton blouse and skirt with a matching bonnet covering her head.

He couldn't imagine Sarah in a simple cotton dress, or cooking, or doing any of the other chores Bee did every day with a smile.

Finally, the women separated and Sarah moved toward him. "Hello, Cole," she said, her bright eyes gazing up at him. "It's good to see you again."

"You too, Sarah," he replied. It was good to see her again. Very good. Because seeing her had given him freedom from the dreams he'd once had. Seeing her again had made him realize she held no power over him anymore. What he'd felt for her once was gone. Completely gone.

Bee had taken her place in his heart, and for the first time since their wedding, he felt like a married man—a man who was ready and more than willing to be a real husband.

He only hoped Bee would be willing to be a real wife.

The touch of Bee's hand on his arm drew him out of his own thoughts. "We should go," she said with a smile. "I'm sure Aunt Meg and Sarah are anxious to rest after their trip."

Suddenly, Sarah grabbed Bee's hand. "That isn't—" she cried out as her eyes landed on the simple gold wedding band on Bee's finger.

Bee grinned. "It is," she said. "Cole and I married the day I arrived."

"But—"

Cole couldn't resist. He wrapped his arm around Bee's shoulder and squeezed. "We sure did, and I couldn't have asked for a better wife."

Cole noticed Sarah's face had paled. Had she expected him to wait until she changed her mind? "Oh…" she murmured, then straightened. The smile creasing her lips didn't reach her eyes. "In that case, congratulations."

"Thanks," Cole said. "Now, let me help you up and we'll go."

They'd brought the four-seater buckboard he'd

bought a few months before, and once he helped the ladies to climb up, he got in and they set off.

"My, you've done well for yourself, Cole," Aunt Meg commented when Bee pointed out the expanse of the ranch. "I'll admit I'm surprised."

"It's so much bigger than I imagined," Sarah put in.

Cole tried to squelch a grin. He couldn't help wondering if her answer to his proposal would have been different if she'd seen the ranch first.

Aunt Meg was resting in her room and Cole was out with Quinn and the others doing their chores. That left Sarah and Elizabeth alone for the first time since their arrival.

"I can't believe you're really here." Elizabeth took Sarah's hand and ushered her to the couch in the main room. She perched on the edge and faced her sister. "I can't believe you're really here," she repeated. "I've missed you so much."

"I've missed you, too, but now we're together again, at least for a little while."

"I hope you stay for a long visit," Elizabeth said. "We have room—"

"I noticed that. This is a lovely home," Sarah said, her eyes drifting around the parlor. "It's small, but so cozy. And the ranch is far more impressive than I expected. I didn't realize Cole was so wealthy now. You made a good match for yourself, sweet."

"Compared to some of the ranches out here, he's not wealthy at all, but he's a good provider and we're not poor," Elizabeth pointed out.

"You're married to a good man, Bee."

"He is a good man, and I thank God every day for him. He doesn't love me, but I can live with that."

"If you'd stayed in Summerton, you wouldn't have married for love, anyway. And at least he's close to your own age," Sarah pointed out, letting out a sigh. "You have no idea what it's been like since you left." She leaned closer to Elizabeth and glanced around to make sure no one was within earshot. "Now that you're not there to share Aunt Meg's attention, her mission to marry me off has become unbearable."

"No," Elizabeth gasped. "It didn't occur to me that—"

"It's not your fault, although it would have been so much easier to deal with if you were there to commiserate with."

"I'm sorry. I didn't realize she would be even more anxious to find you a husband."

"You were so brave to leave when you did."

"I didn't want to leave without telling you, but I was afraid you'd change your mind and decide to marry Cole."

"I did change my mind," Sarah said softly. "Aunt Meg was relentless, and finally I realized I would have no life until I was married. The thought of spending my life with one of those stuffy old men…" She exaggerated a shudder. "I decided Cole was the lesser of two evils."

Sarah wanted Cole!

Elizabeth rose and crossed to the window. Puffy clouds dotted the clear blue sky and the sun glistened off the mountain peaks in the distance. "So you came here to marry Cole," she murmured.

"That's right," Sarah said to her back. "I did."

Elizabeth spun around to face her sister. "But what about me?"

"I honestly didn't think for a minute that he'd actually marry you."

At least Sarah was being honest, Elizabeth thought. Still…

"Don't worry , Bee," Sarah said, approaching her and taking her hand. "I know I could have him if I wanted him, but I'd never want to hurt you. Now, how about that tea you were making?"

Elizabeth nodded absently and moved to the kitchen. While she prepared the tea, Sarah stayed in the parlor, chattering about their journey, the people they both knew back east, and all the news she assumed Elizabeth would be dying to hear.

Elizabeth barely heard any of it. Her heart was breaking, because for the first time in her life, she wasn't sure she trusted her sister.

"You amaze me," Aunt Meg declared when she laid her fork down and folded her napkin and set it on the table after supper that night.

Cole had invited Quinn to join them for supper, and four pairs of eyes focused on Elizabeth's aunt.

Elizabeth had set out china and silverware that Cole had told her belonged to his grandmother. Silver candlesticks cast a soft glow on the snow-white tablecloth, and fresh flowers in a vase decorated the center of the table.

He'd had everything stored when he went off to fight in the war, and had sent for it after he built the ranch house, knowing that Sarah would expect to live the way she had in Summerton.

Elizabeth was satisfied with the table. In her opinion, it rivaled the dinner table in Aunt Meg's house back east.

She'd cooked a slab of beef complete with roasted potatoes and vegetables, fresh bread and butter she'd churned the day before. The cherry pies in the oven were browning beautifully, and she'd made clotted cream to go with them. She'd even found a special tea blend in the mercantile that she knew her aunt favored to round out the meal.

If she had to say so herself, the meal was perfect. She couldn't think of one thing her aunt could criticize her for.

"Not only did you go off without a word and travel half way across the country, but you've surprised me more times today that I could ever imagine," Aunt Meg began.

Elizabeth's stomach dropped. She loved her aunt dearly and she'd always seemed to disappoint her. She'd hoped that this visit would show her that she'd grown up. It seemed she'd wished for too much.

A slow smile creased Aunt Meg's face and the laugh lines at the corners of her eyes deepened. "And I couldn't be more pleased. I'd almost given up on you becoming a proper young lady. And such a good cook, too. That meal was every bit as good as Mrs. Doughty's." She rested her hand on Elizabeth's arm. Her smile turned conspiratorial. "Even better than Mrs. Doughty's, but next time you come home, don't tell her I said that."

The warmth and love in her aunt's voice filled Elizabeth with happiness. Heat colored her cheeks at the compliment. "Why…thank you, Aunt Meg."

"It seems Bee had quite a few secrets," Sarah put in. "Wherever did you learn to cook?"

"Most of the dishes I made tonight were from Mrs. Doughty's recipes," Elizabeth said with a giggle. "Mrs. Doughty taught me to cook whenever you both were out, usually when you were shopping because we knew you'd be gone for hours."

Aunt Meg's eyes widened. "I don't believe it. I don't recall her asking permission to allow you into the kitchen. I'll have to have a talk with her when I get home."

"Believe it, Mrs. Main," Quinn put in. "Trust Bee to find some way to get what she wants," he added with a laugh.

"Please don't be angry with her, Aunt Meg," Elizabeth said. "I made her promise not to say a word."

"Mrs. Doughty was always very protective of her recipes." Aunt Meg dropped a cube of sugar into her tea. "I'm surprised she was willing to share them."

"She didn't," Elizabeth admitted. "Not really. Before I left, I copied the recipes when she wasn't looking."

Aunt Meg's eyes crinkled in amusement. "Oh, my goodness. I'm sure she'd have apoplexy if she knew that."

"It seems Bee kept quite a few secrets from us." Sarah smiled sweetly at her as she lifted the china cup to her lips and took a sip of tea.

Elizabeth met her gaze. Had there really been a sarcastic tinge to Sarah's words, or was she letting her imagination run away with her?

"She may not have told you her plans, but I'm glad she came. I couldn't ask for a better wife," Cole put in. "I don't know how I ever managed without her."

Elizabeth cast him a curious glance, but said nothing. What had gotten into him? Was he trying to make Sarah jealous? Make her sorry she hadn't accepted his proposal?

She rose and hurried into the kitchen. She heard a

chair scrape against the floor and a few moments later, Cole was standing beside her at the stove.

She reached into the oven and took out a cherry pie. "Do you need something?"

He shook his head, wrapped an arm around her and planted a kiss on her lips. "You outdid yourself tonight, Bee."

Then he turned and went back into the dining room, leaving Elizabeth standing in the kitchen, the cherry pie burning her hands even through the thick towel wrapped around them, and her legs feeling as liquid as the pitcher of cream on the counter beside her.

Something was wrong with Bee. Cole had sensed it for the past three days, ever since her aunt and her sister had arrived. He'd expected her to be happy, to enjoy having company, particularly Sarah. He had no idea what could be causing her to be so quiet and distracted. It wasn't like her at all.

Quinn had taken Aunt Meg and Sarah into town, and Cole and Bee were finally alone. And he was determined to find out what was going on. He'd noticed she seemed distant with her sister, and he couldn't help wondering if they'd had a disagreement.

He found Bee in the garden, furiously pulling weeds from between the rows of ripening tomatoes.

"I want to talk to you," he said, coming up to stand

beside her. He noticed the sun had darkened her hands, something her aunt would never have allowed to happen if she'd still been back east.

She looked up, her bright blue eyes filled with concern. "What is it?"

"I want to know what's wrong."

"What's wrong with what?"

"Not what. What's wrong with you. You haven't been yourself since Sarah and your aunt got here. Did you and Sarah have an argument?"

"No. Of course not."

"Then what's bothering you?"

She turned away from him and tugged at another weed. "Nothing."

The denial came out far too quickly.

"I know something's wrong, and I really wish you'd tell me so I can help you to fix it."

"You can't fix it," she said softly.

"I can try—"

"Please," she said with a quiver in her voice, "just go back to whatever you were doing and let me finish weeding the garden. I can't tell where the weeds end and the vegetables begin."

He nodded. "Okay, but when you're ready to talk about what's bothering you, I'm here." He turned and walked away.

So he was right. Something was eating at her, but she wasn't willing to share it with him. He was sure it had something to do with Sarah, but they'd always been close. He'd never heard of them ever having a cross word between them.

Was Bee upset that Sarah was here? Was she worried that he might have lingering feelings for Sarah?

A few weeks ago, he wouldn't have been able to deny it. But now, now that he'd seen Sarah again, he knew without a doubt that Bee was the woman he loved, the woman he was destined to spend his life with.

He'd tried to show her how much she meant to him, to make her feel special. But he'd never said the words. Maybe it was time to say the words, to tell Bee how important she was to him and how much richer his life was now that she was in it.

He didn't want to say anything while Bee's aunt and sister were still visiting. Sarah had told him the day before that they were planning to leave soon to go to Texas for a visit with her aunt's younger brother.

He'd tell Bee after they left that he'd fallen in love with her. If she didn't believe him, he'd have to somehow find a way to convince her that she was the woman he wanted, not Sarah. After everything that had happened, and the history the three of them shared, he only hoped he wouldn't have to.

Elizabeth was miserable. Supper times were the worst. Even though Sarah and Elizabeth had always been able to read each other instinctively, in this case Sarah didn't seem to notice Elizabeth was unusually quiet, while Aunt Meg was oblivious to the tension around the table.

Cole, on the other hand, had been going out of his way to compliment her on everything from her meals to how pretty she looked. Several times, she'd heard him tell Aunt Meg how glad he was that he'd married her.

On the surface, it looked like Cole was finally starting to care for her. If they'd been alone, Elizabeth would have been thrilled.

Instead, she grew more and more suspicious that Cole was merely trying to make Sarah jealous at her expense.

Elizabeth and Cole rarely had any time alone

together now that Sarah and Aunt Meg were there, and Cole tended to find one excuse or another to wait until Elizabeth had retired for the night before he came upstairs.

Sharing a bed with Cole, feeling his warmth beside her and wanting to be a real wife to him but knowing he wanted another woman, was torture.

Anger and sadness warred within her until finally, one afternoon she decided it was time to clear the air. If he wanted Sarah, she needed to know.

Cole had said he'd be out in the north pasture fixing a broken gate. Aunt Meg was resting, and Sarah had taken the buggy to go into town.

She wrote a note and left it on the dining room table, then changed into a tan riding skirt and boots, then hurried to the stable.

For a second or two, she wondered if what she was doing was wise. She'd never ridden that far from the house before, and Cole had often mentioned how easy it was to get lost.

She could wait for Cole to get home, she supposed. The thought disappeared as quickly as it came. The sooner she got this over with, the better.

As Elizabeth saddled the mare Cole had given her when she first arrived, she made a decision. She had to offer him his freedom.

She wasn't sure exactly where she was going, but since the sun streamed through the kitchen window in the afternoon, she knew which way north was.

She rode slowly, letting Bluebell take her time while her tears fell freely. The sun shone brightly overhead, the sky a deep azure blue without a cloud to mar the vastness of it. Still, although it was the middle of summer, the sun glistened on a few patches of snow still clinging to some of the mountain peaks. The sounds of nature calmed her somewhat—birds twittering overhead, the gurgle of the water washing over the rocks in the river beyond the stand of cedars nearby, the rustle of squirrels and other small animals skittering through the trees and high grass.

She'd thought she could be content with his friendship, but after seeing Cole and Sarah together, she realized she couldn't live her life taking second place in his heart.

She reined in the mare and brushed her tears away with the sleeve of her blouse. Squinting into the sun, she searched for some sign of Cole.

He wasn't there. She was sure he'd said he would be in the north pasture. Perhaps he'd ridden over the ridge for some reason. Flicking the reins, she rode on until finally, she gave up. There was no sign of him anywhere.

Turning, she rode back in the direction she'd come, expecting to see the ranch house in the distance at any moment. Instead, she saw only emptiness as far as the horizon.

Where was the house? Had she somehow lost her bearings and ridden in the wrong direction?

She looked up at the sky. The sun had shifted until it rested like an orange ball on top of one of the mountain peaks. How long had she been riding?

And where was she?

She drew on the reins, a sliver of panic rising in her chest. The sun would be setting soon, and already the heat of the day had lessened a little, but not enough to make her cold. Yet.

Twisting in the saddle, she looked around her. Trees, empty pastures, ridges of stone.

She was lost!

Elizabeth was frightened. She didn't know where she was, and there were no landmarks to guide her. She'd been riding for what felt like hours, and with every minute, her fear rose.

Stop it, she chastised herself. Panic won't help. You have to think logically.

She drew her mare to a halt and gazed around. Nothing but high grass, brush and trees surrounded her.

It was late afternoon. She knew the sun set in the west, and the river that ran through the ranch was east of the house. As long as she kept the sun at her back, eventually she'd reach the river.

She'd started out riding north, but she had a feeling she'd ridden in circles and was completely disoriented now.

Feeling much calmer now that she had a plan, she flicked the reins and set off. Several times she wondered if she'd made a mistake, and as dusk fell, panic was setting in again when she finally heard the gurgle of water.

A sigh of relief escaped her lips as she guided the horse to the river's edge.

While her mare drank, she crouched beside the water and scooped up a few handfuls of water for herself.

She looked around. She had a decision to make. North? Or south? The right one would take her home. The wrong one…she'd be spending the night in the wilderness.

Already the temperature had dropped, and she rubbed her arms to generate a little warmth. And with every passing minute, it got darker. She didn't have the luxury of time to decide.

The mare turned to face her, her huge brown eyes looking at her expectantly, as if to ask where they were going. Climbing back into the saddle, Elizabeth made her decision. "Well, Bluebell," she said to the horse, "I'm going to hope we're still north of the house. So take me home."

Cole kicked the dried mud off his boots and opened the front door. Usually, the clamor of pots and pans met his ears and the aroma of supper cooking filled his nose. Today, for the first time since Bee had arrived, there was neither.

Sarah looked up from the linen tablecloth she was embroidering. "Where's Bee?"

"Isn't she here?" Silly question, he thought a second later. If she was there, her sister wouldn't be asking.

Sarah shook her head. "She left a note saying she was going to find you."

He hadn't seen any sign of her while he was working. It hadn't taken as long as he'd thought to mend the fence in the north pasture, so he'd gone to help Pete and TJ putting up hay for the winter. "I haven't seen her. What time did she leave?"

"I don't know." Sarah set her embroidery down. "Aunt Meg went to rest early afternoon. I got restless so I borrowed the buggy and went into town. I'm sure I wasn't gone more than two or three hours. When I came back, she was gone."

Cole glanced at the grandfather clock. "So she's been gone almost four hours."

A knot formed in his stomach. Something was wrong. She'd come to find him for some reason, and likely ridden to the north pasture. So why hadn't she come home when she'd seen he wasn't there?

The sun was sinking behind the mountains. It would be dark soon, and she was out there alone. The temperature dipped at night, too, and she likely didn't have anything with her to keep warm.

If something happened to her…

"I'm going to look for her." Grabbing his hat off the hook behind the door, he jammed it on his head. He'd already opened the door when Sarah appeared beside him and laid her hand on his arm.

"If you'll saddle a horse for me," she said. "I'll come with you."

He turned to look at her. Fear shone in her eyes and her forehead was wrinkled in a frown. He understood she was worried, too, but he wasn't feeling particularly sensitive to her feelings right then. "No, Sarah," he said. "There isn't time to saddle an extra horse for no reason. It'll be dark soon and if I don't find her before then…" He let his words trail off. His chest squeezed tight at the thought of Bee out there, alone, in the darkness, with no food or water. Or protection against the bears and coyotes that roamed at night...

"But I want to help—"

"I know you do, but I don't have time to worry about you keeping up."

"I can ride—"

"Unless you've changed a lot in the past six years, you don't ride well."

She rested her hand on his arm. "But—"

"I'm going alone," he said. "I'll find her and bring her home."

Sarah gazed up at him, her head cocked to one side the way she always did when she was thinking hard.

Then she smiled. "You love her now, don't you?" she asked quietly.

He stepped out onto the porch and turned back to face her. "I do," he said. "Honestly, I didn't at first. When I married her, I was hurt. And angry. I waited for you all those years. I worked my fingers to the bone to be able to provide a life for you. It couldn't match what you'd be leaving, but I hoped it would be enough to make you happy. I loved you and stayed faithful to you for six years."

"I know." Sarah's voice was soft, seductive.

"And just when I thought I'd have everything I ever wanted, Bee showed up. Do you have any idea what that did to me?"

"I never meant to hurt you…"

He smiled then. "I believe that. And now, it doesn't matter, because I love her now more than I ever thought I'd be able to love anybody again. It looks like I married the right sister in the end."

"She's loved you since she was barely old enough to realize there was a difference between men and women," Sarah told him.

His eyes widened. "She has? How did I not know this?"

"Because you didn't want to see it, I suppose," she said. "Have you told her how you feel?"

He shook his head. "I just realized it myself. I'm going to tell her eventually, but I have to find her first."

Elizabeth was so relieved to see the ranch house that she almost burst into tears. "There it is, Bluebell. We're home."

As if the horse sensed her anxiety—or maybe it was her own anxiety for shelter and food—the mare shook her head and began to trot over the fields, moving faster and faster the closer she got to home.

As Elizabeth rode into the yard, she noticed the barn door was open. Quickly, she dismounted and led the mare toward the opening.

Light from a lantern hanging on a nail cast a soft glow through the barn. Voices met her ears.

Sarah's voice. And Cole's. And he was telling her how much he'd loved her.

Her heart tumbled into her stomach. She'd tried to put her suspicions out of her mind on the long ride home, but she'd failed. Sarah had been gone part of the afternoon, and Cole wasn't where he said he'd be. Were they together? Were they rekindling the relationship they'd shared for so many years?

She stepped into the opening. Sarah and Cole were standing together near the far end of the barn. As she watched, Sarah moved closer to Cole and rested her hand on his arm.

Seeing them together as she'd seen them so many times over the years was like a knife in her chest. A gasp escaped her lips while tears stung her eyes, threatening to spill over.

She took a step back. She had to get away, to be alone.

Too late.

"Bee!" Cole's voice filled the space as he hurried toward her. "Are you all right? Where were you?"

Sarah rushed over and threw her arms around her. "We were so worried that something had happened to you."

"I'm fine," Elizabeth replied shortly, forcing the words past the thickness in her throat. Drawing herself out of her sister's arms, she turned to Cole. "If you wouldn't mind taking care of Bluebell, I'll go and start supper."

She spun around and walked off as calmly as she could manage even though her heart was breaking.

Elizabeth hung the towel on a hook beside the sink. It was time to accept the truth—Cole still loved Sarah. And as Elizabeth had always done in the past, she might as well face him now and find out what he planned to do.

Cole was in the barn checking the animals before he retired for the night, so Elizabeth picked up a woolen shawl and wrapped it around her shoulders.

"Where are you going, dear?" Aunt Meg asked, looking up from the book she was reading.

"I'm going outside for a few minutes, Aunt Meg," she replied. "I won't be long."

It wouldn't take long. It was very simple, in reality. One question. Did he want her to leave? A simple answer—yes or no.

Her heart thudded in her chest as she walked across the yard to the barn.

She'd almost reached the door when she heard Sarah's voice inside. "You should tell her tonight."

"I'm not sure—"

"The sooner she knows, the better," Sarah said.

Ducking out of sight, she plastered her back to the outside of the door. Her body shook with sobs she wasn't able to hold back.

She had the answer to her question.

She'd known this day might come, and she'd thought she was prepared for it. But now that it was here, she knew she'd been fooling herself for years.

Cole loved Sarah. It was that simple. And no matter what Elizabeth did or how good a wife she could be to him, he couldn't control what his heart wanted. He couldn't choose who to love any more than she could.

She could move away, could pretend she hadn't heard the words that were tearing her heart to shreds and destroying the dream she'd had for so many years.

What would be the point? She'd have to face the reality eventually, so she might as well get it over with.

Stepping into the soft glow from the lantern inside the barn, she paused and looked at them, her twin sister and her husband.

Cole saw her first. "Bee," he said, coming toward her. "What's wrong? You look like somebody died."

Not somebody, she wanted to say. Something. Her marriage.

"I'll leave you two alone," Sarah said, quietly moving past them toward the opening. "I'm sure you have a lot to talk about."

"We do have a lot to talk about," Cole said once Sarah had disappeared into the night.

Bee's hands were clenched at her sides, her lips in a thin line. She was having a hard time holding herself together.

"Are you sure you're all right?" he asked. "You're so pale and you're shaking. Maybe I should take you back into the house and make you some hot tea—"

She couldn't bear to listen to his sympathetic words any longer. Swallowing past the grief closing her throat, she croaked out, "Please, just say what you have to say so that I can start making plans."

His brow creased. "What are you talking about?" he repeated. "What kind of plans?"

"What I'm going to do," she replied quietly. "Where I'm going to go."

He closed the gap between them and gripped her upper arms. His gaze bored into her, piercing her with its intensity. "Why are you leaving? Wait a minute. Are you leaving me?"

"Isn't that what you were going to tell me?" she asked. "That you and Sarah want to be together? That you want me to go?"

"What?" His voice grew louder. "Where did you get a silly idea like that?"

She raised herself to her full height and faced him squarely. "Don't deny it. I heard you and Sarah discussing it. I heard her tell you that you should tell me tonight."

He released her so fast she stumbled backward for a moment before she regained her balance. He took a step back and raked his fingers through his hair, shaking his head as his gaze never left her face.

Then he started to laugh, a loud booming laugh that filled the barn. "Oh, Bee…"

Anger overcame the sadness filling her. Her tears came then, rolling down her cheeks and dripping off her chin to the dirt floor. She stormed toward him, her eyes sparking with unbridled fury. "Do you find this amusing?"

Suddenly, he wrapped his arms around her and drew her close. The scent that was so uniquely Cole's filled her nose. His heartbeat pulsed against her ear. His warmth washed over her.

"I'm sorry I'm laughing. You're just so wrong."

"I'm not wrong," she insisted. "Don't lie to me. I heard you tell Sarah you loved her."

"I did tell her that."

The words speared her.

"I did love her," he repeated. "I don't now."

She pulled back until she could see his face. "You don't want her?"

He shook his head. "I don't want Sarah. I want you. Now and always."

"What?" she said again, unable to believe she'd really heard the words she'd waited to hear for so many years.

"I did love Sarah. I won't deny that. And I wanted to spend my life with her. And when you showed up instead of her, I was hurt. I was angry. I thought it didn't matter who I married because the woman I loved didn't love me back."

Elizabeth waited, sensing he had more to say.

"Now I know that what I felt for her wasn't real love," he said, "not the kind of love I have for you. I love you, Elizabeth Susan Main." He lowered his head and kissed her. His lips were soft at first, then more demanding.

She clung to him, her heart racing, heat streaking through her veins. Could it be possible that her dreams were coming true?

Her mind whirled as the kiss went on and on until finally, he broke away, his breathing ragged. "I don't want you to leave," he said, his voice breaking.

"But…Sarah…she came here to marry you," she began. "She told me she could have you if she wanted you, but that she wouldn't take you from me."

"She was wrong. So very wrong. She can't have me. No one can have me but you." He smiled. "She might have come here to marry me, but not because she loves me. And now, she knows I love you, and she's happy for us."

"She is?"

He nodded. "Your sister wants to be married, but she wants what we have, too."

"I thought when you said all those nice things to me that you were trying to make her jealous."

"No. I was trying to show you how I felt about you, but I should have just said the words instead. I'm sorry if I upset you."

She gazed up at him. A smile creased his face, and love shone in his eyes. "I have a confession to make."

His smile faded. "What is it? You're not going to tell me you two have been tricking me again, are you?"

"No, but it would have been fun to do it just one more time."

"Bee!"

She grinned. "I promise we won't ever do that again."

"Good. Now what's the confession?"

"I didn't come to Colorado to marry you because I wanted an adventure and to escape Aunt Meg."

"You didn't? Then why—?"

Finally, after years of keeping silent about her feelings for him, she could say the words she'd longed to tell him. "I came because I loved you. I was sure that if we married, I could be a good enough wife that eventually I could make you love me. And even if you didn't, I thought I could be content to be your second choice."

"You aren't—"

She smiled. "I know that now, but when I saw you with Sarah again, I knew I couldn't live my life that way, knowing your heart belonged to someone else. And when I heard the two of you talking, I thought you were planning your future together and that you were going to tell me you wanted her instead."

Cole chuckled. "Silly goose, she knows how I feel about you and she was prodding me to tell you. And now you know."

"I do. We were always friends, but knowing you love me and I love you makes it even better."

He nodded. "It does."

He kissed her again, soundly and passionately. Her heart soared and the tears fell, but this time, they were tears of joy and happiness.

EPILOGUE

Elizabeth and Sarah stood together on the boardwalk in front of the Wells Fargo office while Cole spoke with the stagecoach driver. Aunt Meg had gone to the mercantile to buy a few things they'd need on their long journey home.

"I wish you'd both stay longer," Elizabeth said. "I'm going to miss you so much."

"We've stayed far too long already."

"It's only been—"

"Three months," she pointed out.

The time had gone by so fast, Elizabeth mused. Having Sarah in Rocky Ridge meant that Elizabeth had had to reveal her true identity and the circumstances of her marriage to Cole. The confession resulted in a minor scandal, but it died within a few days, mainly due to how well-liked they both were and the fact that it was obvious they loved each other very much.

Cammie, Agnes and her other friends found the whole situation very romantic, especially when Sarah assured them she had no feelings for Cole.

"We've stayed far longer than we planned to," Sarah went on. "But now I have to go back home with Aunt Meg and likely marry one of her choices."

Elizabeth gazed along the street as three men on horseback rode into town. She recognized them as some of the men who worked for Cole.

Three *unmarried* men.

She spun around and grabbed Sarah's hands. Excitement filled her. "No, you don't!"

"What?"

"You don't have to go back." Elizabeth couldn't contain her excitement. "You can stay here. We have plenty of room and—"

Sarah chuckled. Wrapping her hand around Elizabeth's, she peered at the simple gold band on her finger. "No, sweet, we can't. In the first place, you and Cole need to build your life together without us getting in the way."

As Elizabeth opened her mouth to protest, Sarah held up her hand to stop her. "In the second place," she went on, "while the ranch is so pretty and it's lovely to gaze outside and see the trees and the mountains, I couldn't live there. It's far too quiet."

"Then we'll find somewhere in town for you to live. Virginia and Will Morgan run a boarding house. They might have room." Elizabeth squeezed Sarah's hand. "Oh, Sarah, please say you'll stay."

"Well…"

At that moment, Cole came out of the office. Crossing to where Sarah and Elizabeth were standing, his gaze slid between them. Aunt Meg joined them a few seconds later.

"What are you two up to now?" Cole asked. "No more switching identities, I hope."

The two women giggled. "No," Elizabeth said. "Nothing like that. I'm trying to convince Sarah to stay in Rocky Ridge."

"But only if there are other handsome men out here who are looking for a wife," Sarah said. "Not a rancher, though. I know you two are quite happy out in the wilderness with nothing but animals for company, but I need to be somewhere civilized."

Elizabeth hugged Sarah, her heart swelling with joy.

"Are there many men in Rocky Ridge?" Sarah asked Cole.

"There are," he replied.

"Then while I'm here, Bee and I will go on a mission to find me a husband before Aunt Meg has a chance to find one for me."

"Why, I never—" Aunt Meg sputtered, but the smile on her face belied her annoyance.

Elizabeth took her aunt's hands in hers. "Aunt Meg? Would you consider staying, too?"

"Oh heavens, no," she said.

Disappointment filled Elizabeth.

"I can't stay," her aunt continued. "I have to go back home…and sell the house first." Her aunt's eyes twinkled merrily. "I can't stay back there without my two favorite nieces."

Elizabeth wrapped her arms around her and hugged her tightly. "That's wonderful."

The stagecoach driver approached. "Your bags are stowed and we're heading out, ma'am. You'd best get in now."

A half hour later, Aunt Meg's stagecoach had disappeared from view, Sarah had been welcomed at Virginia Morgan's boarding house, and Cole and Elizabeth were driving away from Rocky Ridge and heading home.

"Are you sure you won't have a problem with Sarah being here?" Cole asked.

Elizabeth shook her head. "She's my best friend and even though I still feel guilty that I suspected her of trying to take you away from me, you've shown me in so many ways that I have nothing to worry about. And I'll need help in a few months," she added with a smile as she gently caressed her stomach where their child was beginning to grow.

Cole's arm reached around her shoulder. He drew her close and kissed her. Happiness and contentment filled her heart as they rode toward the ranch, looking out across the fields to the mountains rising into the sky.

To their land. Their future. Together.

WANTED: THE PERFECT HUSBAND, the third book in the Rocky Ridge Romance series, is ready for you to read next.

Sybil Franklin needs a husband - fast! So why is Devin McGregor sabotaging her efforts to find one when he's already refused her marriage proposal?

Get your copy now!

www.ingramcontent.com/pod-product-compliance
Lightning Source LLC
Chambersburg PA
CBHW030753200726
48288CB00004B/1152